MARRIED
by
MIDNIGHT

MARRIED
by
MIDNIGHT

Julianne
MacLean

A PEMBROKE PALACE NOVELLA

Acknowledgements

Special thanks to my cousin and critique partner Michelle Phillips (a.k.a Daisy Piper) for your constant support and creative assistance, editor Patricia Thomas for helping to make this book shine, and reader Michelle Whitney, whose lovely gift of needlepoint hangs in my dining room where I write and still inspires me with each new project. Thanks also to my agent Paige Wheeler at Folio Literary Management for thirteen years of excellent representation.

Thanks also to Romance Writers of Atlantic Canada, the Eloop, the Summit Authors and most especially my husband Stephen and my daughter Laura for all the joy and laughter you bring to my life. Lastly to all the readers who have sent me letters and emails over the past few years asking about Garrett's story. Your support and encouragement is what kept my Pembroke Palace fires burning. Thank you!

vi

Prologue

Pembroke Palace, England
Christmas Eve, 1874

*I*T WAS AN intimidating prospect—to make love on one's wedding night with a husband one might never see again—but in a few short hours, the deed would be done.

After listening carefully to the terms of this curious marriage contract, Lady Anne Douglas had agreed to every demand. Today she would speak her vows before God. She would promise to love, honor, and obey her husband until death parted them, so there could be no turning back.

Not that she wanted to turn back. To the contrary, this was a first-rate offer and she had been grateful to accept, for she was known far and wide, throughout the whole of England, as damaged goods. At least this bizarre pretence of a marriage would provide her with a generous financial settlement that would guarantee her independence forever.

Which was why, in a few short hours, she would walk down the chapel aisle to stand at the altar beside Garrett, her future husband, and later she would welcome him into her bed to claim his husbandly rights.

To ensure it was all legally binding.

Anne took a deep breath and let it out. Her heart was galloping like a beast, and she worried she might suddenly change her mind, order a carriage, and bolt. Why?

It was fear, plain and simple ...

Turning away from the snowy landscape outside the window, she paced around the room and labored to steady her nerves. She would not, under any circumstances, entertain the notion that this was a mistake.

Just because her betrothed wanted nothing to do with marriage in the traditional sense did not mean she would not benefit from the arrangement. That was why she chose this path in the first place.

Up until a few days ago, she had been so sure she could manage it ...

A knock sounded at the door just then, and her maid entered with her wedding gown.

Anne's stomach churned with panic, and she wrestled with the most overwhelming urge to break free and flee into the raging snowstorm outside, because heaven help her, she had been very irresponsible these past two weeks.

She should never have allowed herself to fall in love with him.

Chapter One

Three weeks earlier

*A*FTER THE WORST spring England had witnessed in over a century—marked by torrential rains, swelled rivers, and flooded fields that destroyed the summer crops—the country was now frozen solid beneath a hostile blanket of crusty white snow.

It had been a harsh winter that began in early November and seemed to go on without end—for there had been no respite from the fierce, bitter winds and constant spray of sleet and snow. And it was not yet half over.

Sitting by the hearth in her uncle's stone manor house in Yorkshire, shivering beneath her heavy woolen shawl, Lady Anne Douglas was beginning to wonder if England were cursed, for surely this could not be normal.

A sudden blast of ice pellets struck the windowpanes, and the dogs began to bark downstairs. Tugging her shawl about her shoulders, she rose from her chair and crossed to the window. She looked down and saw a large black coach pulling to a halt in front of the house. It was a striking image against the pure white landscape. Not to mention the fact that they'd had no visitors for a month—for who in their right mind would venture out into such abominable weather?

The dogs continued to bark like ferocious beasts in the front hall while Anne watched two gentlemen in elegant black overcoats and top hats alight from the vehicle and hurry up the steps. One of them carried a black leather portfolio.

She leaned forward and touched her forehead to the frosty glass, but lost sight of the visitors as they reached the front entrance. There was some commotion below as the door opened and the dogs were put into a separate room, where they continued to bark and growl.

Who were these men, Anne wondered, and what did they want? It must be an extremely important matter of business to bring them all the way to the outer reaches of Yorkshire on such a bitterly cold day.

ᘓᘏᘙᘐᘗ

A half hour later, Anne was summoned to the drawing room.

Her uncle stood before the fire while the two mysterious gentlemen callers sat in chairs with their backs to the door, facing the sofa. As soon as Anne was announced, they rose to their feet, turned, and regarded her with interest.

She stared back at them with an equal measure of curiosity, mixed with a twinge of concern.

They were both exceedingly handsome with dark, chiseled facial features, muscular builds, and striking blue eyes. Brothers surely, for not only were they similar in appearance, they wore the same expression of inquisitive intelligence.

"Well, don't just stand there," her uncle said, moving closer and dragging her into the room. "Come over by the fire so our guests can get a look at you." He shoved her to stand on the threadbare carpet. "She may not be pure, but I daresay she's appealing to the eye."

The gentleman on the left cleared his throat and gave her a look of apology as he bowed courteously. "Lady Anne, it is an honor to make your acquaintance." He fired an irate glance at her uncle, who blinked at him in the muted gray light fighting its way in through the frosty window.

"What's wrong?" her uncle Archibald asked. "Oh. I have not made the proper introductions, have I? Lord Hawthorne, allow me to present my niece, Lady Anne.

Anne, this is Devon Sinclair, Marquess of Hawthorne, and his brother, Lord Blake, both of Pembroke Palace."

A shiver of apprehension rippled up her spine. These were very auspicious guests indeed. Their father was the Duke of Pembroke, one of the highest-ranking peers in the realm. His palace, filled with priceless art and antiquities, was considered one of England's greatest treasures. Some said their Italian Gardens were so beautiful they brought even the most cynical, hard-hearted men to tears.

Hadn't she recently heard the gardens were damaged?

But what were these illustrious gentlemen doing here at her uncle's manor house, three weeks before Christmas, so far from their home in the middle of a raging snowstorm?

She lowered her gaze and dipped into a curtsy. "Good afternoon."

When she met the marquess's cool blue eyes again, he inclined his head at her, as if studying her temperament.

"Your uncle speaks highly of you," he said.

I doubt that.

She had the good sense, however, not to speak her mind.

Lord Hawthorne gestured toward the sofa. "Will you please join us?"

Her gaze darted back and forth between the two guests and her uncle. They were all staring at her as if she were some sort of odd novelty in a glass case.

"Please, Lady Anne," the other one said, as if he recognized her reluctance and wished to set her at ease.

She studied Lord Blake for a moment, experienced an inexplicable whisper of calm, and took a seat.

"We understand you spent the past four years caring for your ailing grandmother," Lord Hawthorne said. "A dutiful and selfless pursuit," he added.

"It wasn't duty," she explained. "It was love." Her late grandmother—God rest her dear, sweet soul—had been the one person who never judged Anne or mistreated her after her terrible fall from grace.

"We are sorry for your loss," Lord Blake said.

"Thank you."

"Lady Anne was an excellent nursemaid and companion," her uncle added. "As I said before, she may not be pure, but she is loyal."

Anne regarded the marquess steadily. "Do you wish me to be a companion to someone?"

A hush fell over the room. "No," he replied. Then he turned his eyes to the baron. "May I request a moment alone with Lady Anne," he asked, "so that we may discuss this proposition in detail?"

"There's no need for any further discussion," Archibald replied. "I have already accepted on her behalf. We need only make the arrangements, though I would like to have my solicitor involved."

Anne frowned. "Your solicitor, Uncle? What sort of proposition did you agree to? If it concerns me, am I not to be consulted?"

Another tension-filled silence descended upon the room, this time heavy as lead.

Lord Hawthorne stood. "I must insist that you excuse us, sir. It is imperative that your niece understands the particulars. We will speak with her in private."

At long last, her uncle rose from his chair. "If you insist, Lord Hawthorne, I must defer to your wishes. But rest assured that your proposal will not be refused. It *will* happen, whether she likes it or not."

As soon as he left the room, Anne challenged the two men. "*What,* exactly, will happen?"

"Nothing, if you do not wish it," Blake replied. "I assure you, Lady Anne, we are not tyrants, and we have other prospects if you refuse—which is your right—but we wish you to know that you are at the top of our list."

"What list?" she asked, nearly horror-struck by the possibilities.

There was a quiet pause until, at last, Hawthorne answered the question. "We require a practical young woman to marry our brother before Christmas," he said.

"I beg your pardon?"

He took a moment to explain. "Our brother needs a wife, but he does not desire a love match, nor does he wish to enter the marriage mart and begin a complicated courtship. He simply wants a contractual arrangement with a woman who understands the situation and desires the same sort of freedom."

"What sort of freedom are you referring to?" she asked. "I do not understand."

"No, of course you do not," Hawthorne replied. "I fear we have not explained ourselves adequately. Please allow me to tell you everything. This time I shall start at the beginning."

ᘎᘏᘎ

"Did I hear you correctly?" Anne said. "Your father is going mad?"

She could not believe it. The Duke of Pembroke was one of the greatest aristocrats in England. The family had a celebrated history, like no other. The Duchess of Pembroke enjoyed an intimate friendship with the queen.

"That is correct," the marquess replied. "He believes all four of his sons must marry before Christmas in order to thwart a family curse."

"What sort of curse?"

Appearing uncertain how best to explain, Hawthorne paused.

"In the spring," he said, "our father believed we would all be washed away in a flood. Now we are in danger of freezing to death, and he expects the palace to shatter like glass if this weather continues. Under any other circumstances it would not matter, except that he has changed his will to disinherit us if we do not respect his wishes. Thankfully, Blake, Vincent, and I found matrimonial bliss earlier this year, but there is one more."

"Another brother? What is his name?"

"Garrett. He is the youngest, and has been living abroad for a number of years. Until very recently, he refused to yield to our father's demands, for he is not exactly ... *compliant*. But we received a letter from him eight days ago. He has finally agreed to come home and fulfill his duty. He is ready to take a wife and secure all of our inheritances. There is also a substantial sum of money he will receive on his wedding day if he marries in time, so he is motivated."

Anne could not help herself. She laughed out loud. "Why in God's name have you chosen *me*? Surely the son of a duke could have any woman he wanted."

"As I said before," the marquess replied, "he has no interest in a love match. He wants a woman who will not need to be romanced—a practical woman who will agree to perform a charade, so to speak, and who will leave Pembroke Palace when he returns to Greece, shortly after the wedding takes place."

"We will live separate lives?" she said, to confirm her understanding.

"That is correct, but you, too, will have freedom. With the allowance Garrett receives as a wedding gift, and the inheritance due upon our father's death, he will provide you with a lifetime annuity. You will be free to live wherever you please. You could purchase a house in London, for example. Or perhaps you would prefer the country. Either way, there will be funds for a very comfortable living with a house full of servants—for the rest of your life."

Anne took a moment to consider all of this. It was not an unattractive offer. Quite the contrary, she felt as if she had just discovered a buried treasure in the garden. It did not seem real.

"What about children?" she asked. "Would I be expected to bear him sons?"

"No. He is the youngest of four. I am the eldest and my wife and I are already expecting a child."

"Congratulations."

"Thank you." He paused.

"Will the marriage have to be consummated?"

"Yes," he replied. "It must be legally binding to fulfil the terms of our father's will."

Anne swallowed uneasily. "What if I become pregnant?"

Lord Blake cleared his throat uneasily. "All of that is outlined in the contract. If a child is conceived, you may choose to raise him yourself, or relinquish him to the care of our family, whereby he would be raised at Pembroke."

Anne gazed toward the door and wondered if her uncle was outside, listening to these details.

"Do you require time to consider it, Lady Anne?" Lord Hawthorne asked. "Because if you wish to accept our proposition, we have the contracts already drawn up. If you are not inclined, however, we would prefer to know immediately so that we can move on to the next candidate as quickly as possible."

She glanced at Lord Blake, who tapped his finger on the leather portfolio that rested on the table beside him. "The contracts are right here, my lady, awaiting your perusal."

"You don't waste time, do you?"

"No," he said. "Christmas is not long off. We have only three weeks to satisfy the terms of the will."

She rolled the idea over in her mind. "Mmm ... I do see the basis for your impatience. If there is no wedding, you will all be cursed. Financially, at least."

"Indeed."

She folded her hands together on her lap. "What if your brother does not approve of me? Does he know about my sordid past? My shocking reputation?"

She had no illusions about her reputation and her marriage prospects, for she had done the unthinkable four years ago when she ran off to elope with her handsome young tutor. Since then, she had given up all romantic fantasies about her future. Until this moment, she had been fully prepared to live out the rest of her days as a spinster.

"He has already indicated that any past scandals are not relevant," Hawthorne replied.

"He cares only for the money," she surmised. "And his freedom."

"That is correct."

"But why me? Why am I first choice?"

They hesitated. "Because we know our brother. He prefers women with dark features. He finds them attractive."

Anne scoffed. "I thought he didn't want romance."

"Correct. We simply don't want to give him any reason to change his mind. That is all."

She thought about it another moment and imagined herself remaining here with her uncle for the rest of her days.

"Money and freedom can have their uses." She eyed that mysterious black portfolio with growing interest. "I do wish to take a look at your offer, Lord Hawthorne. Will there be any room for negotiation?"

The marquess raised an eyebrow in surprise, while his brother quickly opened the leather case.

Chapter Two

Seven days later

IN THE CRISP early evening air, a heavy crested coach, conveying Lord Garrett Sinclair from the train station, rumbled up the steep hill on its final approach to Pembroke Palace. The young golden-haired lord, who had come all the way from the Greek island of Santorini, was sound asleep inside.

There was neither a breath of wind, nor a single cloud in the sky. The moon's bluish glow glistened upon the ice crystals that shimmered on the surface of the snow, while the sound of the coach wheels rolling over the frozen rutted road remained the only disturbance.

When at last the vehicle passed under the impressive triumphal arch and the horses' hooves clattered over the icy stones on the cobbled court, Lord Garrett woke with a start and sucked in a deep gulp of air.

The dream was always the same ... *The relentless roar of the wind in the sails, the taste and grit of the salt on his lips, Johnny's small wet hand slipping from his grip ...*

Like every other night since the accident, it woke him, haunted him, tortured him—like a violent, spiteful ghost.

Drenched in sweat, shivering in the chill of this punishing English weather, Garrett sat forward and worked to calm his breathing. When would it end? he wondered. Not just the weather, but this terrible torment inside of him. Would he know happiness again? He prayed to God that this Christmas would deliver a gift, a reprieve from the agony he'd endured since spring. Otherwise he wasn't sure he could go on living.

Sitting back, desperate for a distraction from the memory of that day on the water, he cupped his hands to the cold glass and peered out at the courtyard and palace, brightly lit up in the night.

Not much had changed since he quit this house seven years ago. It was still the same ostentatious braggart of wealth and social position—a sickening display of showy baroque architecture with giant towers and turrets, a commanding clock tower over a massive portico at the entrance, and enough steps to intimidate even the most privileged aristocrat—not to mention any decent common man of typical upbringing.

All this belonged to his family alone, while thousands of decent, hard-working people starved in the poverty-stricken streets of London. He wanted no part of this world, yet he needed the funds that his father had offered out of the strange depths of his madness. Garrett had come home to do what he must in order to attain them and put them to good use.

Nevertheless, what he must do plagued yet another part of him, for he supposed he was no better than a whore—selling himself for money—and he feared he was about to marry a woman cut from the same cloth. He didn't know what to expect and was quite certain this was the second lowest point in his life. Not to be outdone, of course, by the first. *Never* to be outdone by that.

The coach crossed the courtyard and pulled to a careful halt at the front entrance. Garrett did not wait for the driver or a footman to open the door. He had been living too long outside this world of class distinctions and chose instead to flick the latch and alight from the vehicle on his own.

Tugging his coat collar tighter about his neck, he stepped out and exhaled sharply. His breath puffed out of him like thick smoke on the chilly night air.

Just then the doors of the palace were flung open, and he braced himself for the enthusiastic welcome he did not wish to receive ... until he saw his sister Charlotte approaching.

His twin.

At the shocking sight of her—so grown up and lovely in her lavender dinner gown and jewels—whatever was left of his long-suffering heart snapped in two.

Heaven help him, this was not going to be an easy Christmas. He wished he could leap forward in time to when it would be over, but that, unfortunately, was not possible. He would simply have to muddle through.

༄

"Garrett!"

His sister ran toward him without shawl or cloak and nearly knocked him over as she launched herself into his arms. Somehow he managed to keep his footing on the icy ground, and held onto her more tightly than he'd expected.

"Charlotte ..." he softly said. "How I've missed you." She was always the one he longed for most.

"And I, you," she whispered in his ear. "Oh, Garrett. I feel whole again at last."

He was vaguely aware of the servants collecting his bags, a footman speaking to the driver. Then all at once the world came back into focus and he found himself stepping out of his sister's embrace to behold the other members of his family. They were all crowded around, shivering in the cold, waiting to welcome him home.

"Mother, it is good to see you." He stepped forward to kiss her on the cheek.

She looked older. Still beautiful, though.

God, his head was spinning. Had it really been seven years?

As he backed away from his mother, he turned to face his two older brothers, Devon and Blake. They had dark coloring and tall, broad-shouldered frames. Like their father.

Garrett, on the other hand—for reasons no one wished to talk about—bore no resemblance to the duke whatsoever. He and Charlotte were golden-haired like their mother.

"You two look well." He glanced toward the palace door. "Is Vincent here?"

"No," Charlotte explained. "He and Cassandra have traveled abroad for an extended honeymoon. We are not certain when they will return. They seemed very determined to enjoy themselves."

Devon stuck out his hand. "Words cannot express how pleased we are to have you home again."

Garrett stared down at his brother's outstretched hand. For a hazy moment, he was overcome by a surprising sense of nostalgia as he remembered the carefree days of his childhood when his father was nowhere in sight and he and his older brothers chased each other through the subterranean passages of the palace and played hide-and-seek in the garden.

Those days were long gone now, however. He knew why they were so pleased to see him, and it had little to do with brotherly affection. They simply needed him to secure their inheritances.

"Don't get too used to it," Garrett replied. "I hope I was clear in my letter. I don't intend to stay long."

An awkward silence ensued.

He met his mother's wounded gaze and felt an instant's stirring of regret. She was a kind woman who had been his greatest protector when he was young, and he bore no ill will toward her, of all people. He would have to do better than this.

"I apologize," he said. "It's been a long journey. I am overtired and out of sorts."

"No apologies are necessary." She slid her arm through his. "Come inside, my darling. It's much warmer by the fire. Are you hungry? I will have a hot supper prepared."

"Thank you." He glanced up at the tall clock tower overhead as they ascended the steps, and it was then that he noticed the duke had not come outside to greet him. He was not surprised.

"Where is Father?"

There was a long pause, as if they each hoped some-one else would provide an answer.

As it happened, Blake was the only one willing to offer an explanation. "He is sleeping. The doctor gave him something to calm his nerves. We won't likely see him until late tomorrow morning."

It hardly mattered. Garrett had no illusions about being welcomed home with open arms by His Grace. The only son the duke ever cared about was Devon, his eldest—and the heir. The rest of them might as well have been born invisible.

Or not at all. Especially Garrett and Charlotte.

A fierce gust of wind blew across the courtyard, and the horses shook in their harnesses. Garrett and the others hurried inside to escape the cold.

A short while later they were seated in the library, crowded around a blazing fire in the hearth. Sparks snapped wildly and flew up the chimney.

Still feeling numb to the bone, Garrett glanced up as Blake handed him a glass of brandy. "You look as if you could use this."

Garrett accepted it with a nod of thanks. He took a sip, then leaned forward to rest his elbows on his knees and collect his thoughts.

"Well?" he said. "Is she here?"

Devon cleared his throat while the others remained silent.

"There is no point dancing around the issue," Garrett continued. "Let us all be frank. I am here to fulfill my obligations and secure our inheritances. I will take a wife—as you have all begged me to do for almost a year—collect the funds that are promised to me, then that will be the end of it. I only ask that we move forward as quickly as possible so I can be on my way."

"On your way? But you must stay for Christmas!" his mother blurted out.

"Yes, you must!" Charlotte echoed.

Devon raised a hand to silence them. "Of course we want him to stay, but there is more that we must explain.

Garrett, you cannot simply marry the girl tomorrow. Father believes our world will come crashing to an end on Christmas Day if we are not all *happily* married. Ever since the incident with Vincent—after that sham of an engagement to Lady Letitia—he believes true love is necessary to thwart the curse."

Garrett frowned. "Are you suggesting I must fall in love with the girl? Good God, I've never even met her."

"No, but Father is under the impression that it is a love match. Otherwise the whole thing is pointless."

"A love match ... ?" His gut turned over with dread. "What lies have you told him?"

Charlotte spoke flippantly. "Oh, what does it matter? He doesn't remember half of anything anyway."

"Charlotte, behave yourself," the duchess scolded.

"I beg your pardon, Mother," she argued, "but you know it's true. We tell him whatever we must in any given moment to keep him from climbing the walls and jumping off the roof."

Garrett drew back with a frown. "Is it really that bad?" He could not imagine his father being anything but in complete control.

"Worse, actually," Blake replied. "Two days ago we found him playing billiards at dawn."

"There is no crime in that."

"He was naked as the day he was born."

"I see." Rather astonished by the image, Garrett swirled his brandy around in the glass and tried to stay focused on the money while he wondered how the hell he was going to manage this charade. It was a vast understatement to say that he had never been close to his father. He wasn't sure what to expect. Would the duke even recognize him, much less believe he was in love with a fiancée he'd never met?

"You must prepare yourself," Devon said. "He is greatly changed."

"He thinks the palace is haunted," Charlotte added. "He gets up in the night, wanders the corridors, and talks to himself."

"To be precise," Devon clarified, "he talks to the ghost of Brother Salvador."

"Who is Brother Salvador?" Garrett asked, shaking his head in disbelief.

"A monk," Charlotte answered.

"He was the prior here actually," Blake added. "When this place was a monastery a few hundred years ago. He was murdered when it was discovered he was having an affair with a woman in the village. That woman is the mother of the first duke, our very own ancestor." Blake's dark eyebrows pulled together with uncertainty. "But you know all of this, don't you?"

"I vaguely remember the stories."

"At any rate," Devon said, "Father will not rest until Christmas has come and gone, and he is assured that the curse has been thwarted. He has instructed his solicitor not to release your marriage settlement until the twenty-fifth."

"That is two weeks from now," Garrett said. "Am I to understand that I must remain here and pretend to be in love with a total stranger until then?"

"She won't be a stranger by the end of it," Charlotte mentioned helpfully.

Good God. He had truly walked through the gates of hell. That reality, along with self-loathing, prickled up his spine.

Yes. He supposed that was rather appropriate, for hell was exactly where he belonged.

"When will I meet her?" he asked.

And did she know about all this? *The naked billiard games? The ghosts and the murders?*

"Whenever you like," Devon replied. "She is in the drawing room presently with Rebecca and Chelsea."

No one said a word for a moment. The tension was as thick as London's fog.

His family was probably terrified he would change his mind and walk out first thing in the morning.

Perhaps he should. He didn't want a wife, nor did he care about easing the woes of a father who had always treated him like the bastard son that he was.

But Garrett's hasty departure would only result in more lives ruined because of him, and he had come a long distance to atone.

Rising from his chair, he moved from the fire to the chilly side of the room where he could take a moment to think. He looked up at all the books on the shelves. A spectacular collection to be sure. Enough to keep one's mind engaged for a lifetime. *A lifetime?*

Marriage was supposed to be for a lifetime ...

But did that really matter? Time and happiness had no meaning to him now. There was nothing but dust in his veins. He didn't care who he married, or how he spent his future. Nothing mattered anyway. Except for one thing. *The money.*

"I will be courteous to her," he said, turning to face all of them. "I will put on a good show for Father, as long as you promise me that the money will be forthcoming on Christmas Day."

"I've checked with Father's solicitors. It will," Devon replied.

"Good. Then I will do what is required."

Bloody hell, he didn't even know the girl's name.

Devon rose from his chair. "Excellent. Then let us go and meet Lady Anne. Follow me to the drawing room. I will introduce you and you can spend some time getting better acquainted this evening."

Wonderful. He could hardly wait.

Chapter Three

*A*NNE IMMEDIATELY ROSE to her feet when the Sinclairs entered the drawing room. The marquess led the way, followed by his sister Charlotte, then the duchess, Lord Blake, and last to enter the room ... their youngest brother, Garrett. Her betrothed.

Dear God, her heart was pounding like a drum. She had watched from the window a short while ago as Lord Garrett exited the coach, but could see little through the darkness and shifting moon shadows. Now here he stood before her, waiting to be introduced.

His skin was bronzed from the sun, his hair thick and wavy—the color of honey. He had full lips, a strong, chiseled jawline and a charming dimpled chin. He was not tall and slender like his older brothers. Instead, he sported a stocky, muscular build. His hands were big and strong, which was not surprising for she had been told he was a master yachtsman.

He lifted his sky-blue eyes and met her gaze. She could not tell a lie. He was, without a doubt, one of the most ruggedly handsome men she had ever encountered. It was madness that he had to *pay* a woman to marry him. *What the devil was wrong with him?*

Lord Hawthorne approached. She was vaguely aware of Rebecca and Chelsea rising from their chairs behind her.

"Garrett, this is Lady Anne."

"It is a pleasure to make your acquaintance, my lady," he said.

He bowed to her, and she gave a polite curtsy while wondering how to proceed from here. What exactly did one say to a beautiful stranger, a stranger one was being *paid* to marry?

༺✿༻

Garrett frowned as he stood before the woman his brothers had selected for him. He had not expected to be wedding such an incredible beauty. She was slender and petite, with striking dark features and sea-green eyes that nearly knocked him over as he walked through the door.

There was something serious and intelligent in those eyes—possibly something a little jaded as well? Or was it greed at the sight of him? Perhaps it was that. She was marrying him for money, after all.

"Would you like to escort Lady Anne to the gallery and show her the family portraits?" Devon suggested.

His brother obviously wished to give them an opportunity to become better acquainted in private.

Fine. Garrett had promised to do what was required, so he would do exactly that. With a polite nod of his head, he approached his fiancée and offered his arm.

༺✿༻

As they left the room, Anne worked hard to settle her nerves. She walked with him in silence down a long vaulted corridor and through a keystone archway, which brought them into a large gallery lit by three enormous crystal chandeliers.

They stopped just inside and looked around at the numerous works of art on the walls.

"I have not been here in quite some time," Garrett said.

Anne was consciously aware these were his first words to her, beyond the initial formal greeting.

"I barely remember what is here," he added.

She took a deep breath and let it out slowly. This was ridiculously awkward, but quite unavoidable. She must simply find a way to push through this uncomfortable beginning.

"Then let us discover it together," she said. "Shall we go left or right?"

"Your choice, Lady Anne."

"I choose left."

They walked the length of the room, stopping briefly to look at each painting, saying nothing as they continued in silence.

On a few occasions Anne would have liked to make a comment or two about the individual pieces, but the tension in the air kept her from venturing forth into easy conversation. She had no idea what was going through this man's mind. If she read him correctly, he was feeling somewhat irritable. And the mere fact of her presence seemed to weigh him down like an anchor.

"This one is very interesting," she mentioned, hoping to draw Garrett out and break through the rigid veneer of ice that stood between them. "I am quite partial to landscapes. What do you think?"

He glanced at the painting without interest, shrugged, then moved on to the next.

Anne's stomach slowly began to tighten with displeasure. The Sinclairs had come to *her*, not the other way around.

The excruciating silence seemed to go on without end, while Anne grew increasingly frustrated. Could she endure this man's reticence for a full two weeks?

Yes. She supposed she could survive anything for personal freedom, but would their performance be convincing enough for the duke? He expected a love match.

"Garrett." Her fiancé's name shot over her lips rather harshly, which was not what she'd intended, but it was too late to take that back. She stopped and let go of his arm.

At last, he spoke. "You wish to say something?"

"I do," she replied, then began carefully. "Clearly this is an awkward situation. For that reason, I believe it will require a certain measure of cooperation on our parts. There is no point avoiding the fact that this is a sham. We both know it, but we must at least put on a good show for your father. I will do my part if you will do yours. Perhaps it would be best to discuss a strategy?"

He glanced about the room as if he needed time to reconsider all this.

"Do you wish to change your mind?" she asked, shocked by the direction this was heading. She had only just arrived. She hadn't even met the duke yet.

Garrett's blue eyes shot to hers. "No, I do not wish that."

"Then could you at least try to be polite?" she suggested.

"I didn't think I was being *im*polite."

"You've barely spoken two words to me since we left the drawing room. Let me ask you again, Lord Garrett. Are you uncertain about this? If you are, tell me now, because I have no intention of *dragging* you to the altar. I am not that desperate."

Though she *was* desperate, for she simply could not face the idea of returning to her uncle's house, and she'd already begun to fantasize about her new life. She'd made plans in her mind—plans that included a modest, cozy little house in Oxford ... or perhaps Bath.

Garrett's eyes narrowed. "We hardly know each other, Anne, and already we are knee deep in an argument." He began to slowly pace.

"This is not an argument."

His eyebrow raised in question. He glanced over his shoulder at her, as if to say *you're still arguing.*

Anne took a deep breath and wondered how best to reply, for clearly Garrett had more than a few reservations about this situation.

"I am certain it will work out swimmingly," she said, working hard to sound reassuring. *"If* we resolve to help each other. I am not sure how much talent I possess as an actress, but I am willing to do what I must to convince your father that we are happily betrothed."

Garrett glanced up at an enormous portrait of a rather fierce looking aristocrat, then took a seat on an upholstered bench against the wall beneath it.

"I apologize," he said. "Please come and join me."

He leaned back against the wall. She sat down beside him, and waited for him to speak.

"I understand what you are saying," he began at last. "When I present you to my father, we cannot appear to be strangers. If he asks, we must know things about each other."

"I agree." Ah, this was better. Now at least they were getting somewhere.

"Tell me something personal," he said, looking away in the other direction, as if this were torture for him. "What do you like to do? When were you born? And where did we meet?"

Anne took a moment to consider how best to stage this production—where to place the props and block the actors. "I believe it would be best if we kept the untruths and inventions to a minimum. Let us simply tell him that your brothers introduced us."

"But I have been out of the country for seven years," Garrett replied, "and Father knows it. We will have to say we met in Florence or Rome. Have you ever been to Italy?"

"No, I've never been anywhere."

He glanced at her suspiciously, as if she had done something wrong. "Why not?"

"Because I have been living in seclusion in Yorkshire for the past four years. I was caring for my grandmother, who passed away six months ago."

There were other far less noble reasons for her seclusion, however.

Did he know about that?

"Did your brothers tell you *anything* about me?" she asked.

"Not really."

"And you didn't bother to enquire?"

He glanced away impatiently. "I thought they made it clear in the contract that there would be no courtship between us, and we would live separate lives."

"Like strangers. Yes, they made that abundantly clear to me, but I thought you might wish to know who you would be marrying. I confess I am curious about *you*."

His brow furrowed with what appeared to be fatigue. "There is nothing to know," he replied. "I am doing this for the money, plain and simple. Once my inheritance is secured, I will leave England and return to Greece."

She sat back and spoke dispassionately. "I see. How wonderful that we have something in common then, for money is my motivation as well."

They sat in chilly, censoring silence. *Good Lord.* Talking to him was like wringing blood from a stone.

"You asked me when I was born and what I like to do," she said, forcing herself to continue, for she wanted that damned house in Oxford and was not about to let him spoil those plans by intimidating her. "I am four-and-twenty. My birthday is March 28th. I like dogs and horses. I enjoy riding. It has been my favorite pastime all my life. I also like to read. I play the piano and can sing reasonably well, and I am very independent. I crave freedom."

"For purposes of this charade," he said without enthusiasm, "who are your parents, and have I met them?"

"My father was Viscount Stanley. You haven't met my parents because they are both dead, which is why I have been living with my uncle, Baron Penrose."

He contemplated that for a moment. "With whom shall we say you traveled to Florence? That same uncle?"

"My uncle would never take me abroad," she replied with a scoff, "but since we are telling lies, and to satisfy your father, let me say yes. It was he."

Another chilly silence ensued while they each pondered the fictional scenario that was finally taking form.

He glanced down at her hand and stared at it for a moment. "I see you are wearing a ring. Is that ... ?"

"Yes, it's my engagement ring," she replied, lifting her hand to give him a closer look at the oval-shaped ruby surrounded by diamonds. "Your brothers gave it to me when I signed the contract. They said it belonged to your grandmother."

He stared at it for a few second more, but made no further comment. A short while later he said, "I suspect we will have to make things up as we go along. Who knows what questions Father might ask."

"I will do my best to be convincing and will share what I tell him."

"As will I," he replied. "When did your parents die? How old were you?"

She regarded him without flinching. "My mother died when I was nine years old, and my father passed away four years ago. I was twenty. That's when I went to live with my uncle. And all that is the truth — not invention."

He paused. "I am sorry about your parents."

She was surprised by his kind words. "Thank you." She lowered her gaze to her lap. "Now you know the most relevant details about me. What should I know about you? For purposes of the charade, of course."

He shrugged, as if there were nothing to tell, before painting a few broad strokes to satisfy her. "I spent the past seven years living in Italy and Greece," he said. "Sailing my boat around the Mediterranean. I also write poetry."

"Have you had anything published?"

"No."

When he offered no further information, she said, "I thought writers were supposed to be articulate, yet you seem to be a master of one word answers."

"I apologize, Lady Anne," he replied, looking her square in the eye. "I don't enjoy talking about myself."

She stared at him for a long moment and frowned at his reticence. *What in the world had caused it?* He was a strikingly handsome nobleman who lived a life of leisure, sailing around the Mediterranean. Shouldn't he be full of reckless charm and good-natured appeal?

"I wonder why I fell in love with you, then," she said. "For the purposes of the charade, of course."

He gave her a dark look. "Because I am the son of a duke with a large financial settlement forthcoming to me. Is that not enough for a viscount's daughter?"

A throat cleared in the doorway just then, and they both turned.

Lord Hawthorne approached. "I apologize for the interruption," he said. "Father has surprised us all by joining us in the drawing room. He seems in good spirits. He wishes to see you, Garrett, and to meet your Lady Anne."

They both stood up while Anne wrestled with a sudden rush of anxiety, for other than a few sweeping superficial details, she still knew very little about Lord Garrett. She did not feel ready to meet the duke.

"Shall we?" Lord Garrett coolly offered his arm.

She had no choice but to accompany him. As they walked together she sensed a similar anxiety in him, for he was about to reunite with a father he hadn't seen in seven years. A father who—according to family—was well on his way to madness.

Chapter Four

"*M*Y SON. GOOD heavens, look how you have grown." Garrett was taken aback by the significant aging of his father since they last parted. The duke was shockingly thin. His hair was pure white and gone wild about his face—and those were just the physical differences.

The duke had been a harsh parent all his life and had never shown any love to Garrett, but now he approached with arms outstretched.

Garrett was intensely aware of Lady Anne stepping aside to give them room to embrace. The shock of his father's warm welcome was enough to make Garrett wonder if he had fallen down the rabbit hole.

"My dear, dear boy." The duke wept as he squeezed Garrett tightly. "I feared I would never see you again, but you have come home to us at last." As he recovered his composure and wiped his eyes, he stepped back to hold Garrett at arm's length. He grinned mischievously. "And with a lovely fiancée, I am told?" He nudged Garrett in the ribs. "Where have you been hiding this little one, eh? She looks like an angel. Introduce me if you will, before I dash off to marry her myself!"

The rest of the family laughed at the duke's teasing tone, but there was an obvious discomfort in the room, as if they all feared he might take hold of Lady Anne and actually do it.

Still shaken by his father's affable behavior, Garrett turned to his betrothed. "Father, allow me to present Lady Anne Douglas."

She fell into a proper curtsy. The duke took hold of her hand and helped her rise. "My word," he said, "but you are an absolute angel. How lucky my sons have been to marry such lovely creatures. Garrett is the last now, but certainly not the least, for he is the one who will break the curse. It's all up to you now, my boy. Isn't that right?"

Another hush fell over the room, and Garrett felt a stirring of unease at his father's high expectations. Was there a veiled threat in it?

You're useless. You'll never be anything but a bloody bastard. Get out of my sight, boy. I can't even look at you.

Garrett pushed the memory down and focused on the point of all this, and why he had come home. The money. He would say and do what he must to secure it.

"Indeed," Garrett replied. "On Christmas Day, everything will be put to rights. You'll see."

Yes. To rights—for I will be well on my way back to Greece by then with a substantial piece of your vast fortune in my possession. And you will never have to see me again. Just as you always wanted.

The duke turned to Lady Anne and offered his arm. "Why don't you come with me, my dear? We shall sit by the fire and sip claret, and you can tell me all about your home in Yorkshire."

"I would be delighted, Your Grace." With a charming smile, Anne accompanied the duke to the chairs in front of the fire while Garrett watched her with a hint of concern, for surely she must feel as if she had fallen down a rabbit hole as well?

She gave no evidence of that, however, as she began to converse with his father. She smiled dazzlingly and laughed at all the things the duke said.
At one point the duke reached forward and kissed her hand. It appeared she had captured his heart completely in the first few minutes of their acquaintance.

If he even had a heart ... Garrett sincerely doubted it.

"Well? What do you think of her?"

Garrett turned to his brother Devon who handed him a glass of sherry. "You chose well," he said. "Father seems to like her, and she is a beauty, to be sure." Garrett raised the glass to his lips and took a drink. "Makes me wonder, though."

"Wonder what, exactly?"

Garrett frowned as he continued to watch her in the dancing firelight. She was not just another pretty young lady. There was something particularly enticing about her—a beguiling charisma that made it difficult not to stare.

"What the devil is wrong with her?" he replied. "One would think a woman like that would have been snatched up on the first night of her first season."

"Perhaps you should ask *her* about that," Devon replied as he set his glass down on a table. "You will have plenty of opportunity tomorrow. We've organized a sleigh ride and an afternoon of skating at the lake."

Garrett continued to watch Lady Anne converse easily with their father. "So there *is* a reason, then," he replied. "A blemish on her character. I shouldn't be surprised, for she and I are both selling our souls to the devil this Christmas. Does Father know?"

"No, and we intend to tell him nothing. All that matters is that you sign the marriage certificate by midnight Christmas Eve, then Father will rest easily in his old age and our family's fortune will be secured."

Lady Anne turned her enormous dark-lashed green eyes toward Garrett just then, and smiled. Her open gaze and astonishing beauty caused a spark of excitement in his core, which caught him off guard and caused him some discomfort—for he had certainly not come home to enjoy himself.

∽১৩৩৩

The snow was covered in a thin sheen of sparkling ice the following day when all the members of the family exited the front door of the palace. Four horse-drawn sleighs had been brought up from the stables and were lined up in a row, waiting to carry them to the lake house for ice skating and hot apple cider.

Anne gathered her heavy wool cloak and scarf tightly about her neck and pressed her hands deeply into her fur muff. The temperature was well below freezing. She could see her breath like tiny puffs of smoke on the air, but there was not the slightest breath of wind.

One of the horses tossed his head and stomped his heavy hoof on the frozen ground, impatient to get under way as Anne and the other young ladies—Rebecca, Chelsea, and Charlotte—approached.

"Each sleigh carries four people," Charlotte explained, "but you and Garrett shall have this one all to yourselves. Father insisted."

Anne glanced across at the duke, who was stepping into the first sleigh. As he sat down, the duchess laid a fur blanket over his lap. He clasped her hand and kissed her on the cheek.

Anne was touched by the affection she saw in his eyes, and the blush that colored the duchess's cheek.

Garrett was the last family member to arrive. Dressed in a fur-trimmed greatcoat and elegant top hat, he came skidding across the icy drive with his hands outstretched as if on a wheel, to balance and guide him.

Charlotte laughed at him. "You're going to end up on your backside if you're not careful!"

He skidded to a halt and slammed into the side of the sleigh. "That's slippery," he said to his sister, as if Anne were not even there.

She felt rather out of place among all these siblings. She had an older brother, but he and his wife had abandoned her after the scandal and they had not spoken since.

"When was the last time you donned a pair of ice skates?" Charlotte asked Garrett. "I doubt it's a common pastime on those sweltering Greek islands you are so fond of."

"It's been too long," he replied. "I hope I remember how to stop without careening like a cannonball into the bank."

Charlotte touched his arm. "You will be perfectly fine, and what about you, Lady Anne? Are you a seasoned skater?"

Anne sniffed in the cold. "Yes, I enjoy skating very much. This has been a good winter for it. Everything is frozen solid."

Charlotte glanced uneasily at the duke. "Yes, which hasn't helped Father's anxieties at all. But now that you two are finally here, I believe he will rest easier. Let us have a good time today. We are all in need of some laughter. Up you go now," she said to Anne. "Garrett will help you. I am off to ride with Rebecca and Chelsea in the next sleigh. Devon and Blake will bring up the rear."

She hurried to join her sisters-in-law, while Anne's eyes met Garrett's blue-eyed gaze in the chilly midday sunshine.

He held out his gloved hand. "Allow me to assist you."

Anne hesitated. How very attractive he was. Hence, she was not surprised when a shiver of physical awareness moved through her as she slid her fingers across his palm.

Without any effort at all, he handed her up. There was a fur blanket on the red leather seat. She waited for him to sit beside her. After he adjusted the flannel-wrapped bricks she covered both their laps with the blanket.

"It's a fine day," Garrett said, looking up at the clear blue sky. The sleigh lurched forward and the bells jingled on the harness. They began in a convoy, moving across the fields toward the forest, which was blanketed in pure white snow and ice that weighed heavily upon the evergreen branches.

Garrett's profile was relaxed as he looked over the fields and back at the palace.

"Pardon me for saying so," Anne mentioned, "but you seem in much better spirits this morning."

"How so?" he asked, finally meeting her gaze.

"Last night you did not seem happy to be here, or to meet me. I believed you would decide to stay behind this afternoon, but here you are."

"Yes, well, here I am, forced to endure the fresh winter air and cheerful sunshine." There was a touch of friendliness in his eyes this morning, and she was pleased he was making some effort at conversation.

Perhaps this would not be so difficult after all, Anne thought as she looked out over the frozen landscape and felt the vigorous breeze on her cheeks. Perhaps Garrett had merely been weary from the journey the night before. He had traveled a great distance, after all. How could she fault him for it?

"You were very good with my father last night," he mentioned. "I was watching you. You seemed at ease and not the least bit ..." He paused.

"Least bit what?" she pressed. "Do you wish to compliment my acting skills? Was I believable?"

He glanced in the other direction. "Yes, I suppose that is what I was attempting to say. For some reason I couldn't find the right words."

"A poet who cannot find words. That is rather unfortunate."

He regarded her with a surprising hint of amusement.

"You're quite right, Lady Anne. It is. Perhaps that is why I haven't written anything lately. I suspect it is not my true calling."

The driver slapped the leather lines to urge the horse to trot faster, for the other sleighs were slicing through the snow at a very brisk pace.

"Hurry up slowpokes!" Charlotte called out from the ladies' sleigh as they sailed past with bright red scarves flying and bells jingling.

Garrett chuckled with an obvious note of affection for his sister.

"You and Charlotte seem very close," Anne commented.

"We are fraternal twins. Did you know that?"

"I did. Your brothers, Devon and Blake, educated me on a number of family topics. They also told me that your palace is known to be haunted. That it is built upon the ruins of an ancient monastery that was torn apart during the reign of Henry VIII."

Garrett's eyebrows lifted and he looked straight at her. "And that didn't frighten you off?"

She felt rather giddy under his direct gaze as a rush of butterflies invaded her belly. Lord Garrett was strikingly handsome. She found it more than a little unsettling.

"I enjoy a good ghost story," she replied, nevertheless. "And I doubt there's any truth to it. Or perhaps I am too skeptical. Have you ever seen a ghost at Pembroke Palace?"

"Not me, but Charlotte might claim otherwise. Poor girl. We used to haunt the subterranean passages when we were children. It couldn't have been easy for her, growing up with four brothers. She certainly learned to stand up for herself—no doubt about that."

Anne regarded him with interest as the horse pulled the sleigh into the shelter of the forest. Suddenly they were among heavy branches covered in fresh snow that fell in big clumps that plopped around them.

"Why are you looking at me like that?" Garrett asked as he leaned back and rested an arm along the back of the seat. "You seem almost baffled."

"I am merely surprised by your openness this morning, compared to last night," she replied. "You seem like a different person."

He shrugged. "I suppose now that I've met you, I am able to relax a little."
"Why?"

He considered her question for a moment. "I think I was worried that any lady who would agree to a plot such as this would have to be unpleasant in some way, or undesirable, or perhaps possess some secret ulterior motive. I feared she might want to lure me into a real marriage. That has happened to me before, but you don't strike me as any of those things."

Anne spoke honestly. "I told you last night that I am here to gain my independence and freedom, not another yoke around my neck."

His eyes narrowed, as if he wanted to look deeper into her character and study her. Find out why. Perhaps test her. "Yes, but some women say that when they don't really mean it. Deep down, what they really want is a fairy tale."

The sleigh jostled them about as they glided over a small knoll where patches of earth showed through the snow. Anne pulled one hand from her muff and pressed her winter bonnet more firmly onto her head. "It's not that I don't believe in fairy tales," she said, "or want true love for myself one day. I do. It's just not something I felt I could attain."

"Why not?"

She inclined her head a fraction, surprised that he had to ask the question. "Because I have been living a rather reclusive life in Yorkshire. I haven't been to London in years and had no reason to expect or hope that anything would change."

She was acutely aware of his arm resting along the back of the seat while he listened to her explanation.

"Did no one tell you about me?" she asked. "Do you not know why your brothers came to *me* with this proposition?"

He drew in a deep breath and let it out. "I must confess I left everything in their capable hands and preferred to be kept out of it, in the dark. But now that I have met you, I cannot help but wonder why you have chosen this path. You are not unattractive, Lady Anne. To the contrary you are a beautiful and charming young woman, and you seem to have your wits about you. I didn't expect them to find anyone quite like you."

Feeling unexpectedly flattered by his words of appreciation—especially after his behavior the night before—Anne shoved her fists back into her muff and hoped the cold air was enough to hide the rush of heat that suffused her cheeks.

"I don't quite know what to say." She paused and decided the blunt truth was the only option. "Fine. If you must know, there was a terrible scandal about me a few years ago. For that reason, I had no hope of marriage."

Garrett's head drew back in surprise. "I see. May I ask what happened?"

"You may, and I will not hide the truth from you since a contract has been signed and we are to be married in less than two weeks." She swallowed and continued. "I was very foolish and fell in love with my charming music teacher. We ran off together and I fully intended to marry him. When my father discovered our plan, he pursued us and paid my young man handsomely to give me up. My intended was very quick to accept it, which was devastating to me, for I had given up everything to be with him. I thought he felt the same way, but now I realize he was only using me to advance himself. I believe he was hoping that Father would accept our marriage and provide us with an allowance. It did not work out that way, but still he benefited."

Anne was quiet for a moment as she remembered the agony of her heartbreak when her father informed her of her lover's decision.

"Then what happened?" Garrett asked.

Anne dropped her gaze to her lap as she recalled the day she walked into church and the congregation fell silent. All heads turned to look at her. No one would allow her into a pew. She had no choice but to walk out, and never return.

She pulled herself out of that abyss and met Garrett's eyes. "My father disowned me. My brother would have nothing to do with me, and my uncle only took me in to care for my elderly grandmother. The moment she was gone, I suddenly became a terrible burden to him. He is very happy to be rid of me, and I assure you I was overjoyed to leave.

"For that reason," she continued, "your brothers' offer was like a gift from heaven. Now I will be able to afford a house of my own and not worry about my uncle marrying me off to some lecherous old man, which I am sure he would have done."

Garrett inclined his head. "Then I suppose it makes perfect sense that you would accept this proposition. I am pleased we could be of service to you."

"And I am pleased I could be of service to *you*," she replied. "It has all worked out rather well, if I may say so."

He leaned back comfortably and propped a boot up on the opposite seat. "Yes, indeed. I must confess, now that I know your whole story, I feel a great weight lifted. This whole madcap plan is starting to make some strange sort of sense."

Anne nodded. "I suppose you could say that."

They regarded each other with a mutual look of bewilderment, then Garrett leaned to the side to see past the driver.

"I believe we are almost there. I hope Father remembers how to skate."

"He seemed quite lucid last night," Anne replied. "I am sure he will be fine."

The driver pulled the sleigh to a gentle halt in front of the octagonal lake house, and the horse jingled the bells as he shook in the harness.

Garrett stood up in the sleigh and offered his hand. "Shall we?"

As Anne gazed up at his clear blue eyes and full lips, she felt an intense shiver of attraction.

His words played over in her mind: *I feared she might want to lure me into a real marriage.*

Working hard to suppress any curiosity about what it might be like to marry a man like this, in earnest, she placed her hand in his and hopped out of the sleigh, onto the snow.

༄ຉ໒ໆ

The servants had arrived early to clear off a large square of ice for skating and to set up a table inside the lake house with hot, spiced apple cider and sandwiches.

Garrett had not seen the lake house in many years and found himself caught up in a whirlwind of childhood memories—of swimming and fishing with his brothers in the summer, of playing hide and seek in the woods in the autumn months.

Though he had left Pembroke under bitter circumstances and hadn't looked back, he could not deny that there were at least some happy memories here. It hadn't been all bad, but during his time away he had chosen to forget what was good about this place. It had been easier that way. What was the point in missing what one chose to leave behind?

Charlotte entered the brightly lit lake house at that moment and stomped the snow off her boots at the door.

How lovely she had become, with her golden hair and smiling eyes. She was the one person who had remained in his heart at all times—this twin sister who always understood him and shared with him a spiritual bond like no other person in the world.

Life had been easier for her, of course, because she'd been born a girl. Their father never begrudged her existence, yet while Garrett was fourth in line to a dukedom, he could never inherit. If anything happened to his three older brothers, a scandal would result to protect the true bloodline of descent from a bastard heir.

And no one wanted a scandal.

Garrett was startled by a hand on his shoulder. "Father looks better today," Devon said. "I haven't seen him so calm in months. It's good that you came home. I believe you are the missing link."

Garrett shook his head. "I find that difficult to swallow. He always hated me."

"That's not true," Devon argued.

Garrett gave his brother a challenging look.

"Fine," Devon replied. "He wasn't the most affectionate parent where you were concerned, but he seems to have mellowed in his old age. You may find that this strange madness has changed him for the better in some ways. Vincent said the same thing, and they have reconciled completely. This change of mind has brought out another side of Father. His cruelty is gone. He seems grateful to have his family nearby. None of us can help but be moved by how vulnerable he has become—like a child in many ways."

Garrett watched through the bank of windows as his father stepped onto the ice and gained his footing.

"You'll see," Devon said. "Spend some time with him, will you?"

Garrett nodded and continued to look out the window. One by one, his family members donned their skates and glided onto the ice—Rebecca and Chelsea in their heavy skirts, holding their muffs close while Blake offered his arm and skated beside them for the first few unsteady moments.

The landscape was perfectly white and pristine beneath the clear blue sky. It was an exceptional winter day and Garrett found himself reveling in this drastic change from his life on the hot, sun-bathed island of Santorini—a lonely existence most of the time.

Exceptionally empty in recent months, but he couldn't bear to think of that now. He pushed it from his mind.

Lady Anne was next to step onto the ice. Garrett chuckled softly as she bent forward awkwardly and wobbled to and fro. Soon, however, she was skating smoothly around the inside perimeter of the square and laughing with Charlotte, Rebecca, and Chelsea.

For a long while he watched her and thought about their conversation in the sleigh. He was surprised by how candid she had been in confessing about her tarnished reputation. Not many women would admit such a thing, and despite the fact that this engagement was a fraud, he found her to be more open and honest than most other women he had met during his life.

She was not trying to entice him into marriage with her charm; she was instead his partner in crime, so to speak, and he felt rather pleased to have a worldly partner for the duration of this charade. On top of all that, she was a stranger at Pembroke, just like he was. Together they would play out this charade. Then they would each be on their own way.

Lady Anne slipped just then and fell forward onto her knees. Garrett was about to rush outside when his entire family skated to her side. She was back on her feet in no time, laughing at herself while the duke followed her around in circles, anxiously checking to ensure she was unharmed.

Anne took his arm and encouraged him to skate beside her, and all was well again.

With a sudden and surprising readiness, Garrett turned away from the window and moved quickly to fetch his skates and join his family on the lake.

Chapter Five

*A*NNE SKATED WITH the duke for quite some time. Mostly he talked about his great passion for flowers and garden design. He also explained how he had been forced to dig up his beloved Italian Gardens the previous spring to protect them from the floods, which he believed to be part of the Pembroke Palace curse.

Blake and Devon had explained everything to her before she signed the contract, but it was something else entirely to hear the duke describe the situation. He sounded quite convincing and did not appear mad at all, for they had in fact suffered through a terrible spring that year. A number of floods had washed bridges away. There were even a few tragic deaths. She couldn't blame His Grace for feeling frightened, yet it was clear that he was becoming delusional in his old age. Sometimes Anne's grandmother believed Anne to be her own older sister, who had been dead for nearly twenty years.

Anne glanced up when Garrett stepped onto the ice and skated toward Devon. If he hadn't enjoyed winter activities in years, it was impossible to tell, for he moved with incredible ease and speed. The three brothers began to race around the square while the ladies screeched and laughed as they whizzed by.

Anne let go of the duke's arm when he waved a scolding finger at them and shouted, "Now, see here! Someone is going to get hurt!"

Blake immediately stopped and suggested the others slow down as well, then escorted his father off the ice and back up to the lake house for a cup of cider.

Anne caught Garrett's gaze from across the distance and he skated toward her. A flash of heat rushed through her body as he drew closer.

Somehow he was becoming more handsome by the minute. She loved how he moved. He was graceful and strong, so at ease on his skates.

His blades scraped over the ice and sent up a flurry of snow as he stopped before her.

"Are you enjoying yourself?" he asked with a charming sparkle in his eye.

"Yes, and you?"

"Immensely so. Shall we skate together? No doubt Father will be watching at the windows."

Anne took hold of his arm. "Then let us put on a good show for him."

Together they began at a slow pace while the others stood around the center of the square, chatting casually. Then all at once, they left in a group to return to the lake house.

It grew quiet all of a sudden, except for the sound of their blades scraping over the smooth surface of the ice.

"I suppose you are missing your boat," Anne said. "I imagine it probably skates across the water just like this when you are at full sail in a strong wind."

He looked down. "That is a very accurate description, but no, I am not missing it." He said no more about it, and instead changed the subject. "But since you told me about your past and why you decided to accept my brothers' offer, I thought you might be wondering why *I* have chosen this path, instead of doing what most men do at my age—which is to take a wife in an honest fashion."

Anne glanced up at him. "You said you were doing it for the money."

"But you never asked why."

She let go of his arm, skated ahead, then turned to reverse her direction and skate backwards, facing him. "It sounds like you want to tell me, but if you do, I insist you acknowledge that I did not wrestle it out of you, or even ask."

He regarded her curiously. "Why would you insist on such a thing?"

"Because you made it clear that you do not want a bride who wants to lure you into a real marriage. I do not wish to be that sort of woman either, so I shall keep my distance. I will not press you to share too many personal details. That will make it easier for us both to sever all ties afterward."

"You have this very well thought out, Anne."

She skated into the center of the ice and stopped there, out of breath. "Not really."

He followed and skated around her in a full circle.

"I believe my brothers chose the perfect woman for me," he said. "Not only are you beautiful, but you are sensible as well, and I admire that."

She watched him warily. "Don't be too quick to admire me, sir, for I am far from perfect. I am marrying a man for money after all—a man I hardly know. But anything would have been better than the dismal future I faced at my uncle's hands."

Garrett skated to a halt before her. "I am glad you will no longer be at his mercy."

She sniffed in the cold and looked across the lake at the snowy forest on the other side, then met his eyes again. "And still, you have not told me why you want the money. I presumed you simply wished to continue living a life of leisure on the Mediterranean ... but now I am not so sure, because you wouldn't have brought it up if that were the case. I think there is something else to it."

He skated around her again, keeping his eyes lowered, as if thinking about something.

Good God, but he was handsome in the sunlight. Her heart raced with excitement as she watched him.

He stopped abruptly and explained himself. "I lost my boat," he said. "It sank and I ... I lost everything."

"My word," she replied. "Were you on board when it happened? Were you hurt? Was anyone with you?"

He began to skate back and forth again. "I was alone," he explained, "and luckily unharmed, for I was able to stay afloat on a life ring until I was picked up by another vessel a few hours later."

She watched him with curiosity and sensed he was not telling her the whole truth. "Well, that is a relief," she replied nonetheless. "Still, it must have been very frightening."

"It is not something I would care to repeat. I am not even sure I will ever sail again." He looked down at the ice and skated in a large figure eight, skating backwards on the second loop. "Even now I am imagining the dark, freezing water that is swirling around beneath this ice. I keep wondering what would happen if it cracked under us and we fell through. You would probably sink to the bottom in those heavy skirts."

"What a morbid thought," she replied as she looked down as well and imagined it for herself. "Surely your brothers would come to our rescue?"

"I am sure they would." He glanced up at the lake house.

Garrett seemed rather lost in thought and though Anne shivered in the cold, she made no suggestion that they go inside.

"Do your brothers know about your boat?" she asked.

"No," he replied, "and I would appreciate your discretion in that regard, especially with Father. He might think I've brought on another curse, and for the first time in my life I am enjoying being in his good graces."

Anne rubbed her hands together inside her muff where it was toasty warm. "You were a naughty child?" she asked with a hint of humor and mischief, hoping to lighten the mood, for it had turned rather dark. "I would never have guessed it."

For a long moment he didn't answer, then he squinted up at the bright sky. "Not so much naughty as unwanted, but that is a story for another day. Are you cold, Lady Anne? Shall we go and have some hot cider?"

Wishing he had not suggested they join the others at this intriguing juncture, she nevertheless took his arm when he offered it, for she had promised to keep her distance and it would be best to hold true to that

promise instead of risking all and caring too much. Yes.
That would be a dangerous mistake to make.

"That would be lovely," she replied as she skated off
the ice with him.

ᜡ

The following night after dinner, while Anne sat at the
table chatting with Charlotte, Garrett found himself
watching her, entranced by her dark, ethereal beauty.
She was unlike any other woman he'd met before. She
was very open and unashamed about her past trans-
gressions, yet at the same time there was something
pure and unworldly about her. He found it difficult to
believe she could have earned the slightest stain on her
reputation.

But she had. She'd admitted it openly.

Bloody hell, he couldn't keep his eyes off her. He was
forced to remind himself a number of times during dinner that it was a physical attraction best left unexplored,
for he and Lady Anne were in a contractual relationship
together, and the terms of their union had been laid out
very clearly by the solicitors at Mason, Morrison, and
Sangster.

He was to marry Anne Douglas by Christmas Eve;
then he would be free to leave England with no further
responsibilities toward her. All the financial arrangements for her future annuities would be administered
by the same team of solicitors—the very firm that was
handling his father's will, which stated that if all four
brothers were not married by Christmas, the family's
entire unentailed fortune would be bequeathed to the
London Horticultural Society.

And it was more than a substantial fortune. The
Pembroke estate was one of the wealthiest in the country. With it, the Horticultural Society would be able to
cloak the entire south of England in a blanket of tulips
and roses from now until the end of time.

At the image of tulips and roses, Garrett's attention returned to his lovely fiancée seated across the table.

She raised her wine glass to her lips and regarded him over the rim for what seemed a sweltering moment. All at once he found himself uncomfortably aroused and wondered what would happen if he entered into a flirtation with her during these two weeks at Pembroke.

She was not a virgin. Perhaps she would enjoy a brief *amour*. There was nothing in the contract that prevented it. They were, in fact, required to consummate the marriage.

But not until the wedding night of course.

He raised his own wine glass to his lips and met her enchanting gaze a number of times throughout the evening. All the while, he had to fight to keep thoughts of bedding her at bay, for he could not possibly deserve such pleasures.

He was here to do what he must to make amends for the accident—of which he had not told the whole truth—not to plunge himself into another temporary, and no doubt dangerous affair. Besides, he wasn't sure she would be agreeable to such a self-indulgent plan, and he certainly didn't want to disrespect her after all she'd been through. He did his best to purge the idea from his mind.

Chapter Six

GARRETT WAS READING the *Times* and sipping coffee alone in the breakfast room a few days later when his mother entered and stopped just inside the door.

"Good morning," he said as he folded the paper and set it aside on the white tablecloth. He noticed how lovely his mother looked in a sky-blue morning dress with white trimmings. She had celebrated her fiftieth birthday earlier that year, but was still as slim and attractive as she had been in her youth.

"I am sorry to disturb you," she said, "but I thought you might like to meet Dr. Thomas. He has been treating your father since the spring. Perhaps you have some questions you would like to ask?"

Garrett did in fact have a number questions regarding his father's state of mind, for the duke was suddenly a proud and doting parent. Was it simply memory loss? Did he even remember that Garrett was illegitimate?

He finished his coffee and stood. "As a matter of fact, I do have questions. Is he here now?"

"Yes, I asked him to wait in the library."

Garrett followed his mother out of the breakfast room and walked with her along the east wing corridor and down the red-carpeted stairs. The double doors to the library were closed, but his mother pulled them open and led the way in.

"Garrett, this is Dr. Thomas. He has been coming all the way from London twice a week since the spring to tend to the duke. Dr. Thomas, this is my son, Lord Garrett."

The doctor—a handsome older gentleman with gold-rimmed spectacles—bowed to him. "It is a pleasure to meet you, my lord. I understand you have been abroad and only recently returned?"

"Yes, that's quite right," Garrett replied, taking note of the fact that his mother was quietly backing out of the room and pulling the double doors closed behind her. "I've been living in Greece for a number of years."

"But you have come home to marry your beloved. I had the honor of meeting Lady Anne a few minutes ago when I arrived. She is stunning. Congratulations to you both."

Garrett nodded at the compliment and invited the doctor to sit down in one of two wing-backed chairs that faced each other in front of the unlit fire.

"You have been seeing my father since the spring?" Garrett said.

"Yes. When your brother, Lord Hawthorne, returned from America and learned of your father's condition and the odd circumstances of his will, he hoped a diagnosis of some mental incapacity might render the will null and void, but sadly he had been deemed perfectly sane at the time the will was drawn up, so there was no hope of negating it. Though I believe the lawyers are still looking into it.

"From what the duchess tells me," he continued, "I understand you and your three brothers have done what you must to secure the fortune either way. You are the last one to marry and the requirements of the will shall be satisfied. Once that is settled it is more a simple matter of proper medical care ... ensuring your father is comfortable and safe in the final years of his life."

Garrett crossed one leg over the other. "What is the life expectancy in such cases?"

Dr. Thomas gave him a reassuring look. "It's difficult to say. The good news is that your father is extremely healthy in every other way. His heart is strong and he is incredibly resilient. I don't see any reason to be concerned that his days are numbered."

"I see. That is good news." Garrett glanced toward the bright windows and tapped a finger on the armrest.

"There is something else you wish to ask me?" Dr. Thomas said. "Please, Lord Garrett, rest assured that anything we discuss today will be kept in the strictest confidence. If there is something you wish to know about your father's mental capacities, do not hesitate to ask."

Garrett met the doctor's gaze and understood why his mother had retained his services. There was something very capable and trustworthy about this man. And there was something else, but he wasn't quite sure what ...

"Can an illness such as this cause the patient to forget the past, or is it possible my father has changed in his old age and become more ... ?" He wasn't quite sure how to phrase it. "Could he become kinder or more generous and forgiving? Because he is not the same man he was when I left here. I will be honest with you, Dr. Thomas. He always treated me with disdain and sometimes cruelty. Now he acts as if I am his beloved prodigal son. I don't understand and I do not know what to believe. Does he remember who I am?"

Dr. Thomas stared at him for a long moment, then sat forward. "I am sorry to hear that he was not the sort of father you deserved, but I will be frank with you. I do believe that a man can change at any stage in his life. Wisdom and experience will often motivate such a transformation. As far as your father's memory goes—he does forget things, his short-term memory is especially faulty, but he does know that you are his son.

"He has asked about you often over the past few months and has wanted you to come home. At the same time, he is delusional about this curse and the ghosts he sees at night. My advice is that you make the most of these final years and try to find a way to forgive him for his mistakes in the past. Enjoy the man he is now. If he wants to treat you like his beloved son, then *let* him, and after he's gone remember these times together. It might give you some peace of mind later on."

Peace. It was something Garrett could not even begin to fathom, for his head was swimming in regret for his own actions in Greece, not so much those of his father's years ago.

"Thank you, Doctor. You've been very helpful—a voice of reason in all this madness."

Dr. Thomas regarded him with understanding, and something about the man struck a chord in Garrett—something strangely familiar. He inclined his head. "Pardon me for asking, but have we met before?"

The doctor stared at him for another thoughtful moment, then a smile reached his eyes. "As a matter of fact we have. You would have been too young to remember, but I treated you when you were a small child."

"What was wrong with me?"

The doctor's brow creased, as if he were struggling to describe the illness. "It was nothing out of the ordinary. Just a fever, but your mother feared it might be serious. She was very concerned."

"How old was I?"

"You were four." Dr. Thomas looked down at the fire.

"I see. Well." Garrett stood up. "Thank you again, Doctor."

Dr. Thomas stood up as well. "I am happy to be of service. If there is anything else I can do for you, do not hesitate to contact me at any time." He handed Garrett his card. "I promise complete discretion."

Garrett looked down at the card and was thankful to have it. He admired this doctor, and trusted him. Perhaps he would be helpful in other ways, for Garrett often felt he had no one to talk to or confide in—especially since the accident.

He was still surprised he had confessed it to Lady Anne ... Perhaps because she, like the doctor, was an outsider.

As Garrett walked out of the library he contemplated why it was easier to confess things to strangers. He supposed one could say what one wanted to say, and then never have to confront the issue again—for that person would be gone from one's life.

Lady Anne ...

Would he really never see her again after they spoke their wedding vows? Something inside him already regretted that, and wished it did not have to be so—but still, he did not want a wife. That is not why he came home.

❧

The duke and duchess placed their glasses on the silver tray and said their good nights. For a few minutes after they left the drawing room, conversations were quiet. With the help of a bottle it soon picked up again.

"I do not know what to believe," Anne said with laughter as she held out her glass for more of the finest brandy she'd ever tasted. "Charlotte assures me that the palace is haunted and the ghosts are a wild bunch of rogues, but you men say otherwise."

Charlotte, who was seated beside Anne on the sofa, also raised her glass to allow Blake to pour more from the sparkling crystal decanter. "Our ghosts are most definitely a terrible band of scoundrels. I have not set foot in the catacombs for years. Why ... I still have nightmares about those wretched howls, and the dark enclosed spaces that seemed to go on forever with no way out. Many times I thought I'd met my maker down there."

Anne decided to play along. She regarded the men with horrified umbrage but spoke sympathetically to Charlotte. "How dare they presume you were imagining it? I think there is something to these legends. Is it not true that a monk was murdered here?"

Garrett sat down beside her and casually lounged back on the sofa. "Be careful, darling, you are dredging up the shocking details of our family's dark history. We have wicked beginnings, and in fact, ghosts are not at all out of the question. Perhaps we are all better off not knowing the truth."

Darling? The teasing in his voice sent flames of excitement shooting into her veins. She could not help but turn her body in his direction. He was sitting very close and she could feel the thrilling challenge in his blue eyes.

She spoke flirtatiously. "You should know better than anyone that I am not the sort of woman who hides from the truth, no matter how shocking or scandalous. Therefore, I challenge you to prove whether or not there are ghosts, otherwise I'll likely believe it was just you and your wicked brothers taunting your poor sister all those years ago."

She became aware, suddenly, of the others in the room who were staring at them in silence. Anne looked up at them.

Rebecca smiled. "Count me in. I wish to join you in the challenge." She turned to face Devon. "Darling, you have never once taken me into the underground. Your father has gone to bed. Now is the perfect time."

Devon tipped his brandy back and swallowed the contents in one gulp. "Very well, then. If you ladies are brave enough to venture into the deepest guts of this house, how could we not oblige your curiosities?" He turned to Blake and Garrett. "What do you both say? Should we shield them from the otherworldly forces by remaining here in the drawing room, or escort them into the fray and act as their protectors?"

"I say we escort them into the fray," Blake replied, "though I doubt any of them will require our protection. They all seem rather confident."

Charlotte stood up. "My sisters-in-law and soon-to-be sister-in-law do not yet understand what they will be facing when we venture below ground. I think perhaps we should bring that decanter of wine."

Devon immediately picked it up by the neck. "I have it. What else shall we take with us? Think carefully now, in case we do not return for a time."

"What exactly constitutes a time?" Anne asked playfully as she stood up. "Should I bring a change of clothes?"

Garrett moved to pick up a small candelabra. "I do not believe that will be necessary, for you shall have very capable protectors at your side. We shall all emerge unscathed; I am almost certain of it."

"*Almost* certain?" Anne chuckled as she followed him out of the drawing room. "Perhaps this is too great a risk and we should all behave like sensible adults and go straight to bed."

"And let them continue to think I never really heard those ghostly howls all those years ago?" Charlotte argued. "No, I think not. I require witnesses to prove I was not a silly little girl with an overactive imagination. Anne, you believe me, don't you?"

"Of course I do," she replied, linking her arm through Charlotte's and realizing she had not had this much fun in a great many years.

Charlotte picked up a second candelabra from the side table by the door and carried it into the corridor. Together they moved quietly and stealthily to the staircase and descended to the main floor.

"Perhaps we should be doing this in the daylight," Rebecca nervously suggested.

"Then we wouldn't see any ghosts," Charlotte replied, "because they only come out at night. At least that is what Father claims."

Anne, Charlotte, and Rebecca all joined hands to follow the men to the rear door that led out to the old cloister. "We will have to go outside for a moment to cross to the chapel," Devon explained. "It will be cold. Are you ladies prepared?"

"What if the chapel door is locked?" Anne asked.

"It's never locked," Devon explained. "It was always one of Father's strictest rules for as long as I can remember. Prepare yourself. There is a frigid wind tonight." He opened the palace door and the candles flickered wildly as the group dashed outside onto the icy ground of the cloister and ran laughing to the chapel. Garrett was the first to reach the door and he held it open for all of them.

Once inside, they each took a moment to recover from the biting wind on their cheeks.

Anne could not ignore the fact that it was the first time she had set foot in a place of worship since her very public fall from grace.

She glanced uneasily at the others who were smiling and laughing, then looked up at the high arched ceiling and felt a wonderful rush of joy to be there without being judged a harlot.

She closed her eyes and took a few deep cleansing breaths, then opened them and looked around.

It was a small, private chapel that would seat fifty people at most, but it was an inviting space with fine oak paneling and tapestries behind the choir stalls. She slowly made her way up the center aisle, running her fingers over the backs of each empty pew.

A stained glass window provided an ornate backdrop for the altar, but she could not make out the colors or details in the glass for there were only a few candles to light the way.

"What a lovely place," she said, deciding to return at some point to see it in full light. She would be married here after all. It was an almost inconceivable notion.

"I haven't been here in years," Garrett said. "It seems smaller than I remember."

She watched his eyes settle upon the white statue of the Virgin Mary at the base of the arched window and wondered what he was thinking as he held the candelabra high over his head.

Meanwhile Devon had already found a secret door behind the pulpit. He unlocked it with a key that was stored beneath a loose stone in the floor.

"I wasn't sure if the key would still be here," he said, handing it to Garrett who slipped it into his pocket. "Are you ready ladies?" Devon asked. "If you're frightened, it is not too late to change your minds."

"Frightened?" Charlotte replied, aghast. She was the first to join him at the door. "We most certainly are not. In fact, I will go first."

Anne and Rebecca followed, but Anne stopped suddenly when she peered into the darkness. "Oh, my. I didn't imagine anything quite like this."

A steep set of stone stairs led down to the underground tunnels beneath the chapel, but it was pitch black beyond the meagre light provided by their candles. A dank, musty smell reached her nostrils and her heart began to race at the prospect of venturing into those dark unknown depths.

"Perhaps it *would* be better to do this during daylight hours?" she found herself suggesting, just as Rebecca had earlier.

"It wouldn't make any difference," Charlotte replied. "It's just as dark down there during the day."

None of them said a word.

"Where do the tunnels lead?" Rebecca asked.

Devon slid an arm around Rebecca's waist. "The corridors twist and turn, and fork off in different directions. It's rather like a maze down there, but there are only two ways out, as far as we know. Here in the chapel, and another door a few hundred yards away in a thick grove of junipers."

"We couldn't possibly return that way." Rebecca said. "It's too cold outside and we're not dressed for it."

"We will retrace our steps back to this door," Devon replied.

Charlotte turned to explain more to Anne. "Some say the corridor was dug out by the canon who wished to sneak out to meet his lover in the village."

"That's devotion by any standard," she replied. "Imagine how long it took him to tunnel such a distance."

"That's just a romantic legend," Garrett said. "The passages have been here since ancient times, probably as an escape against invading Vikings or Norman conquerors. Though I don't doubt the canon used it to meet his paramour. How else could he have managed the affair without anyone learning of it until the woman gave birth to a child?"

Again they fell silent as they stared down the steep steps and Anne contemplated the lengths the canon had gone to in order to be with the woman he loved.

"Shall we march on?" Charlotte asked. "I am brave enough if the rest of you are."

That was a challenge none could refuse. Anne nodded gamely at her future sister-in-law, and together they led the way.

The deeper they went, the chillier and damper it became.

"What's that smell?" Rebecca asked. "It's rather disgusting."

"It's just your husband," Garrett whispered, and laughed as Devon shoved him into the wall of the stairs.

When at last they reached the bottom, Charlotte held up her candle. "The passageway goes straight for some distance, then it forks to the left and right. Shall we proceed?"

Anne winced as a cold drop of water went plop on her forehead. There were a number of shallow puddles at her feet, but at least they weren't frozen solid.

They continued moving forward together until they reached a T at the end.

"Left or right?" Charlotte asked. "I cannot remember the correct way to reach the other door. It's all very vague in my mind."

"If I remember correctly," Garrett said, "both tunnels lead there eventually, but we might go around in circles for a while before we reach the other side."

"Then we will have to find our way back here," Anne mentioned." With a shiver of apprehension, she glanced back in the direction of the chapel door. "That won't be locked when we return, will it?"

"I have the only key right here," Garrett replied, patting his waistcoat pocket.

"Then I shall stay very close to you," she replied, slipping her arm through his.

"There, you see?" Devon smiled at Rebecca. "You ladies are quite safe with us."

Charlotte elbowed him in the ribs. "Speak for your wife, not me. I am not frightened in the least. Here is what I propose. Garrett and Anne—since you are newly engaged—you must test your togetherness by taking the left corridor, while Devon, Rebecca and I will take the right. The team that reaches the other door first wins."

Garrett held up his candles. "I accept the challenge. Let's go." He grabbed hold of Anne's hand and dashed off to the right.

"Wait a minute!" Charlotte shouted after them. "You were supposed to go left!"

"Too late!" he called over his shoulder. Anne laughed and followed.

As soon as they reached a fair distance, they stopped at another T in the tunnel and paused to catch their breath.

"Which way?" he said, swinging the candelabra left and right, and creating an eerie yellow glow that danced and glistened upon the damp walls. "You choose."

"Let us go left this time," she said. "But look at this." She touched the rough bumps in the wall. "Try to remember this shape in case we end up here again."

"It looks like the letter A," he mentioned.

"You're right." She clasped his hand as he led her down the corridor that was narrower than the first. Eventually it curved to the right and brought them to another fork, where they turned left again.

Anne was enjoying the sensation of his large warm hand wrapped around hers, yet had to remind herself that this attraction she felt for him was not something she should encourage, for soon after the wedding day, they would part ways. She must take care, therefore, to guard her heart from him. She certainly hadn't entered into this agreement to cause herself another broken one.

The corridor slowly narrowed until they were passing through it side-by-side, holding their breath.

"I remember this section," Garrett said. "It will widen again soon. We are on the right path, I believe."

"Wait," Anne said and squeezed his hand. "Do you hear something?"

They both stopped and listened.

"What is that?" she asked as a hot ball of fear dropped into her belly.

They were deep in the underground, trapped in a set of allegedly haunted passageways, and she could barely breathe. Now she was hearing ghostly howls, just as Charlotte had described. "Do you hear it?"

Garrett turned his head to the side to meet her wide-eyed gaze.

The candles danced in a cold draft that snaked around her ankles and drifted up her gown, but none of that unnerved her as much as the gorgeous blue of Garrett's eyes as he smiled at her.

"It's Charlotte," he said. "She is toying with us. Or rather, she is toying with *me*. Seeking vengeance, no doubt, for all the times we left her alone down here and howled like ghosts."

"What terrible brothers you were," Anne replied.

"Yes, we were a bad bunch. Are you sure you want to marry me?"

She couldn't help but smile. "I've never been more sure of anything in my life."

His smile vanished into a frown, and she wished she could pull the words back, for they suggested a romantic devotion she did not mean to convey when it was obvious he had only been teasing her.

"I think I've had too much brandy," she added, hoping it would excuse her remark.

Still, he gave no reply. He merely stared at her for an intense moment before turning to lead them further along the narrow passageway.

At last it widened and she emerged beside Garrett with a sigh of relief. "I'm not sorry to be out of there. How much farther, do you think?"

He held the candles aloft. "I'm not sure. There are a few more turns, and we could end up back at the chapel if we take a wrong one."

"Let us hope luck is with us tonight."

"Indeed," he said, taking hold of her hand again.

The warmth of his touch caused a spark of response in every part of her body.

Together they forged on. They took another left turn, then heard the sound of the wind howling up ahead.

"I believe this is it," Garrett said, moving faster.

Anne held tight to his hand until they reached a small set of wooden steps leading up to an ancient-looking door, barred shut.

Garrett set the candelabra down on the ground, climbed the steps and raised the heavy wooden bar. He shoved the door open a crack, but a fierce wind blew in, so he shut it again and set the bar back in place.

"It appears we are the victors," he said, descending the stairs to join her. It was difficult not to stare at his muscled thighs and hips, and those strong, broad shoulders. Instead, Anne forced herself to glance elsewhere at the damp walls, and shivered. "I wonder how long it will take the others to arrive?"

He immediately shrugged out of his jacket and wrapped it around her shoulders. The warmth and musky scent of his body still lingered pleasantly inside as she slipped her arms into the sleeves.

"Is that better?" he asked.

She smiled and nodded while admiring the impressive contours of his muscular shoulders beneath the clean white shirt and fine tailored waistcoat.

She'd read a lot about sailing large ships and suddenly she was caught up in a romantic fantasy of him standing on the deck of his boat, using those strong hands and powerful muscles to hoist a mainsail, then turn a wheel hard to bring it about while crossing a wide open emerald sea. How heroic he would look, commanding a yacht with the wind whipping through his thick golden hair and the waves crashing up against the hull.

She couldn't bear to imagine the accident, however, and the boat sinking beneath him. What a terrible ordeal it must have been.

"We'll sit on the steps and wait," he suggested and placed the candelabra on a convenient shelf of rock.

The mere sound of his voice sent little tremors of excitement through her body, which she fought to ignore, for she must be very careful. It must be this dark place and her imaginings that were taking her thoughts where they should not be. She was growing more and more attracted to Garrett by the minute.

As she sat down beside him, he slid his arm around her shoulders and pulled her close to keep warm.

She would have preferred to remain indifferent about his nearness and the touch of his steady hand on her shoulder, but it caused a noticeable warming of her blood.

"Are you feeling warmer now?" he asked, brushing his lips lightly across her ear. The moist heat of his breath caused a tingling sensation in her core.

"Yes, that is much better."

But was it? She wasn't so sure.

She couldn't seem to conquer the desire that was now coursing through her body. She wanted to lean closer, to feel his other arm wrap around her too. To feel his lips on hers in this dark cold place.

"Do you think they are taking their time on purpose?" he asked, his voice like warm silk in her ear. "Charlotte seemed particularly eager to send us off to be alone together."

"Maybe with all their ghostly howls, she expected me to throw myself into your arms and beg to be held."

His lips were soft on her cheek as he spoke with gentle allure. "I wouldn't have objected if you had."

The implications of that statement aroused her senses to an alarming degree. She couldn't help but look up at him, and when she did, she became instantly lost in those moody blue eyes and the idle way his hand was stroking her shoulder.

His gaze dipped lower to her lips and held there for a sizzling moment of contemplation.

Anne was shocked at her own eager response as he lifted her chin and slowly touched his lips to hers. Shivers of delight followed the lush heat of the kiss, and her body went weak all over. If not for the chill in the air, she might have fainted from the searing pleasure that came next as his lips parted and his tongue swept inside.

Her body melted. He let out a husky groan of need.

His passion caught her completely off guard, for he had been so cool and distant in every other way. She was confused by the change, but had no will to resist, for it was deliciously wicked and he was the most wonderful kisser.

Garrett stroked her cheek and turned his body to lift her onto his lap.

"Your lips are like sweet honey," he whispered with a smile, tasting her lightly and kissing down the side of her neck.

An exotic euphoria poured through her, though she was not entirely comfortable with any of this. She had been seduced once before with dreadful consequences, for she had given herself to a man before marriage and did not wish to repeat that mistake. It didn't matter that she'd signed a contract. They were not yet married, and anything could happen between now and then.

A ghostly howl echoed through the underground and the candles flickered in the draft that blew in under the door.

"I think they'll be here soon," Garrett calmly mentioned as he kissed down the front of her throat.

"That's probably a good thing," she replied, tilting her head back to allow him greater access, "because we really shouldn't be doing this."

"Why not?" he asked. "I see nothing wrong with it. We are engaged to be married."

"In name only," she reminded him. "And just because I was ruined once does not mean I am an easy conquest."

There. She'd said it, and she was glad she did, for she did not wish there to be any misunderstanding.

Garrett's hand stilled at the small of her back and he slowly blinked, then drew back and beheld her with some concern. "I never thought that."

"No?" She posed the question as a challenge, for she would not be taken advantage of. "Are you sure about that?"

The voices and laughter grew closer.

He didn't have a chance to reply before she slid off his lap to sit on the step beside him.

Her cheeks flushed with heat. Anne took a moment to touch her hair and make sure everything was in order, but felt Garrett watching her.

"Forgive me," he said. "I didn't plan to kiss you, but I swear on my life, you are the most beautiful woman I have ever met."

Taken aback by the passion in his words — and the frustrated desire that was clearly evident in his eyes — she was barely conscious of the others rounding the last corner and appearing before them, out of breath, with candles blazing in the darkness.

"Upon my word!" Charlotte said, staring at them on the steps. "You two look like you've been waiting for hours! You must have chosen every turn correctly."

"It appears we have been soundly defeated," Devon added.

"Was there to be a prize?" Rebecca asked.

Garrett rose to his feet and spoke with easy humor, which completely masked the intense emotion he'd revealed to Anne just now. "We never discussed that, did we?"

She was thankful for the distraction, for she was still reeling from the kiss and feared everyone would see the indecent wantonness in her eyes, and regret their choice of a bride for Garrett.

"A prize ..." Charlotte said, gazing down at Anne, who had not yet risen to her feet. "It should be the lady's choice. What would you like, Anne? A special cake prepared in the kitchen tomorrow? Or perhaps Garrett should buy you something. A pretty bauble?"

"But he is a winner, too," she declared. "He shouldn't have to present me with anything. I will therefore choose the cake as prize—something we can all enjoy." She turned to him. "Do you like chocolate, Garrett?" she asked him.

He wet his lips, and heaven help her, she melted all over again. He smiled.

"Very much so." He helped her to her feet and their eyes held for a few heart-stopping seconds before he turned to address Devon. "Getting out of here is another contest entirely. Do you think we'll make it back to the chapel before dawn?"

He was still holding her hand, and her whole body tingled with awareness at the warmth of his flesh and the discernible might of his large, strong hand, wrapped snugly around hers. Everything about him was so very male and invigorating.

Then he let go, and the connection was broken. A single breath sailed out of her.

Anne watched him lead the way out and felt a powerful surge of lust as she recalled what he had said: *I swear on my life, you are the most beautiful woman I have ever met.*

It was flattery, nothing more, she tried to tell herself, and she must remember that she had been led astray by pretty words once before.

Nevertheless, as she followed the others out of the catacombs and through the church, then across the cold courtyard, and into the luxurious warmth of the palace, she was overcome by an unfathomable wave of joy that left her feeling bewildered.

It had been ages since she'd felt part of anything, and this family, that had so warmly welcomed her into their fold, was like a force of nature. There was so much history here, so many secrets she could sense ... but did not know the answers to. Life had been difficult here, yet there was laughter.

She had forgotten what it felt like to be playful, as she had once been in her childhood.

And tonight she had trusted Garrett enough to allow him to hold her in his arms, to kiss her, and flatter her. She had allowed herself to feel desire. And she was unsettled by the fact that her body still burned for more.

Chapter Seven

"*I* AM QUITE CONVINCED there is an attraction between them," Charlotte said as she spooned a poached egg and a slice of ham onto her plate at the sideboard.

Rebecca and Chelsea were already seated at the table finishing their biscuits.

"I think so, too," Rebecca replied. "It was quite obvious last night when he took her hand and dashed off into the darkness with her the instant you suggested they should be partners. And when we found them at the end, Lady Anne was blushing. There can be no doubt about it."

Charlotte sat down at the table and spread her napkin on her lap. "Do you think anything happened between them? A kiss perhaps?"

Chelsea sat back with her coffee and exhaled on a sigh. "Now I am disappointed I went to bed so early. It sounds like I missed a great deal of excitement."

"Not at all," Rebecca replied. "Though it was more than a little amusing when Charlotte howled like a rabid wolf."

"Not a wolf," she explained. "I was the inconsolable ghost of a murdered monk who was separated from his great love."

Chelsea laughed. "Ah. Well, that is not nearly half so bad. Were you trying to frighten them?"

"I was having my revenge on Garrett for all his shenanigans when we were children ... But you are both missing the point. What do you think about Garrett and Lady Anne? Is there any chance they might truly fall in love and decide to pursue a real marriage?"

Rebecca sliced into her ham. "If that happens, it will be higher forces at work to be sure, for I know that was not Devon's intention when he and Blake searched the whole of England for a suitable bride. They were specifically looking for a woman who would be content with the pretense of a marriage, not a real one."

"Not just be *content*," Chelsea added. "They were looking for someone who was also seeking independence. I believe Anne is that woman."

Charlotte regarded them both shrewdly in the morning's winter light beaming in the windows. "That may have been their intention, but I am beginning to believe father's curse is not really a curse at all, but some sort of magical boon. So far, three out of my four brothers have all been muscled into matrimony against their will, and all have found their perfect mates. You are both blissfully happy, are you not?"

Rebecca and Chelsea agreed.

"*You see?* I think Garrett may also be on the verge of discovering the same sort of happiness. He has been away too long and for that reason has forgotten all of us. Now I believe he is remembering happier times. And Anne is wonderful, isn't she? They are a strikingly handsome couple and seem to possess similar dispositions as well. They enjoy talking to each other and there is an undeniable spark of attraction between them. Have you noticed? I certainly have. I think it is only a matter of time before they realize they are madly in love with each other, and he will decide to stay here at Pembroke where he belongs."

Rebecca sipped her coffee. "Perhaps you are right. You are his twin, after all. You know him far better than we do. But I also think you should be careful not to get your hopes up."

Charlotte lifted her gaze. "What do you think, Chelsea?"

When Chelsea smiled she was astonishingly beautiful, warm as the sun. "I think you are a born matchmaker, Charlotte, and Garrett will have to watch out if he wants to hold onto his bachelor lifestyle after the wedding day."

Charlotte dug into her poached egg. "I don't believe I will have to do much of anything, except watch this so-called curse take its natural course. Those two are meant for each other and he is most certainly *not* meant to return to Greece."

Rebecca and Chelsea shared a hesitant glance.

"Watch," Charlotte said. "You will soon see that I am right. Come Christmas Day, he won't be going anywhere because he will be blissfully happy in the arms of his beautiful new wife, and all will be exactly as it should be."

The clocked chimed on the mantel, and Charlotte ate her breakfast with gusto.

০৬২৩০

Garrett could not sleep. He lay tossing and turning for nearly two hours wondering what the devil he had gotten himself into—agreeing to marry a woman he'd never met for the sole purpose of collecting his inheritance. He'd thought it would be a simple affair.

The lady in question had agreed to the terms of the contract, which was to live separate lives after the wedding day. He therefore expected to avoid any awkward romantic situations with her, yet here he lay as randy as a schoolboy because he had taken her into his arms the night before and kissed her sweet honey lips until he couldn't think or breathe.

God help him. She really was the most beautiful creature he had ever encountered, and his body was still throbbing and aching with desire—which was not part of the plan.

Anne had made it clear she did not wish to become entangled in a sordid affair—and thank God for that, for he certainly didn't want to desire her or heaven forbid fall in love with her. But he did want the money. Just the money.

A noise in the corridor caused him to sit up in his bed. What was it? A groan? A sob? It sounded eerily like one of Charlotte's ghostly howls in the underground passages. Was she playing tricks again, or had the spirit of a murdered monk truly come to haunt the Sinclairs?

Tossing the covers aside, he slipped out of bed, pulled on his dark green silk night robe, tied the sash, and moved quickly to the door. With a gentle click, he turned the knob and peered into the dark corridor.

Another tragic sob echoed off the walls and Garrett quickly shut his door. His heart pounded like a hammer. Bloody hell, what was wrong with him? He didn't believe in ghosts. He certainly was not afraid ...

This was ridiculous. It had to be Charlotte.

Quickly lighting a candle and picking up the brass holder, he pulled the door open and burst forth into the corridor to look left and right.

The candlelight cast peculiar shadows across the floor as he swung it around. There was no one about—and damn his heart for beating so fast.

He took a moment to catch his breath and think about what to do. If he had any sense in his brain, he would go back to bed and ignore Charlotte's tomfoolery ... but if he did that, he'd only be plagued by more lustful thoughts of Lady Anne and her soft, warm lips, and he'd spend more hours tossing and turning in bed and driving himself completely mad.

Hearing another distant, hollow moan, he turned in the other direction and caught a flash of white moving toward the stairs.

If that were a ghost, he'd eat his nightshirt.

With swift, determined strides, he hurried to the end of the corridor and held the candle aloft. "Hello!" he called out. "I know you're there. I saw you."

A chill draft blew across the floor. He heard the heavy creaking of a door and was about to threaten this mischievous ghost with physical violence when he saw what appeared to be a bright silky glow. His stomach dropped. Then he heard a voice.

"Garrett, is that you?"

Christ. He really needed to get some sleep.

"Yes, it's me. Is that you, Lady Anne?"

She was dressed in a white silk robe and carried a flickering candle as she approached. Her wavy black hair was long and loose about her shoulders. He nearly fell over at the sight of her, so beguiling was she in the golden light.

"I heard howling and moaning," she said. "After last night, I confess I've been a bit spooked. I couldn't sleep."

"Nor could I," he replied. "Have you been skulking about in the corridors? Was it you I saw a moment ago?"

"What do you mean?"

He gazed at her for a strange, shivery moment that seemed to pulse through his veins. "I saw someone running . . . I think. Someone dressed in white."

She turned the other way. "It couldn't have been me. I only just came out of my room this moment." She gestured toward the door. "This is my room, right here."

He turned to glance at it.

At least now he knew where she slept—a necessary piece of information for the wedding night when he would enjoy the pleasure of consummating the marriage.

All of a sudden he lost himself in a fantasy of removing her nightdress and running his hands over those sweet, naked curves. The wedding night would be a great pleasure indeed.

Anne gazed at him for a lingering moment, as if unsure what to do. Perhaps she had recognized the lust in his eye and was concerned he had come here to seduce her. It was not an unreasonable assumption after the way he behaved the night before.

In an effort to ease her mind, he let out a soft chuckle. "I believe Charlotte is up to something."

Anne's shoulders immediately relaxed and she exhaled a breath. "Ah, that makes sense. Thank heavens. I was beginning to think this place was truly haunted, and I'm not sure I could have held on to my courage until Christmas."

She shivered and rubbed a hand over her upper arm.

"Are you cold?"

"A little. Thank you, by the way, for lending me your dinner jacket last night."

"It was no trouble," he replied, wondering what would happen if he offered her his robe now and invited her back to his room to sit by the fire and sip some brandy. He let his gaze roam leisurely down the length of her lovely body. No matter how hard he tried, he couldn't seem to keep from imagining all sorts of wicked, sensual delights.

"And we won the race," she quickly added, as if struggling to fill the silence so he couldn't suggest a chancy drink by the fire. "I quite enjoyed myself."

"As did I. The cake was delicious tonight." For a fiery instant he wasn't sure if he could wait until the wedding night to touch her again. His desire for her was palpable, like some sort of erotic drug taking over his senses.

When his desires began to feel more like some form of torture, he decided it was time to say goodnight and return to bed, but another moan caused them both to jump.

"Did you hear that?" Anne asked.

Garrett raised his candle high over their heads. Together they hurried to the end of the corridor and spotted another flash of white heading into the south wing.

"It's my father," Garrett said. "He must be having some sort of episode. We should get him back to his room."

They both hurried to pursue him.

"Father, wait!" Garrett shouted as they drew closer. "Let us help you!"

The duke halted and swung around. His face was ghostly white and creased with a wretched look of terror. He dropped to his knees and cupped his hands together as if in prayer.

"Are you all right, Your Grace?" Anne asked, kneeling down beside him and laying a hand on his shoulder.

"I couldn't find my way back," he replied. "I'm so frightened."

"There's nothing to be frightened of. We'll help you."
Garrett pulled his father gently to his feet.

Anne and Garrett walked on either side of the duke,
quietly leading the way.

"Did you have a bad dream?" Anne asked.

The duke regarded her with confusion. "I don't know.
I can't remember."

They walked in silence until they reached the duke's
door and all three entered the chamber.

"Everything will be all right now," Garrett said as
he helped his father into bed and covered him with the
blankets.

The duke's stricken eyes darted back and forth
between the two of them. "It's so cold outside. There is
a curse on the palace, you know. If it freezes, the palace
will shatter like glass."

Garrett took hold of his father's hand. "Do not fret
about the curse," he said. "Anne and I will marry on
Christmas Eve and everything will be fine."

His father inched down and rested his head on the
pillow. His eyes were wracked with fear. Still mystified by
this radical change in him—for the duke was not same
man—Garrett stroked his forehead and hair.

"Where's Adelaide?" he asked. "My sweet wife?"

"She's sleeping," Garrett replied.

"Will you stay until I fall asleep?" his father pleaded.

"Of course," Garrett replied, while meeting Anne's
concerned gaze on the opposite side of the bed.

She moved forward to hold the duke's other hand. He
fell back to sleep within minutes, and Garrett's heart
felt heavy like stone.

ᘒᘞᘒ

"He never looked at me that way before," Garrett whispered as he quietly closed his father's door. "He seemed
so desperate and helpless."

"You were very kind to him," she replied. "He's a lucky
man to have such good children."

They started down the corridor together to return to their own separate bedchambers.

"It feels odd," Garrett said. "I've been gone for many years and I've hated him for as long as I can remember. I didn't want to come home. I didn't care about the Pembroke fortune being lost to the London Horticultural Society. This estate meant nothing to me. But now that I am here, it's like I am seeing everything for the first time, and I have a different father. He is not the same man he once was. To be honest, I like this one better."

Anne took hold of his hand. "Then it is good that you have come home. Perhaps it will help you to resolve whatever stood between you in the past."

He was overcome suddenly by a profound compulsion to explain to her exactly what had been standing between them. Did she even know?

"How much did Devon tell you about my relationship with my father?" he asked.

"Nothing, really," she replied. "I was told only that you had no wish to live at Pembroke—or anywhere in England for that matter. That you wanted to live a separate life, unconnected to your family."

He held the candle over their heads as they rounded the corner and reached her door. He was vastly disappointed to end their conversation. They both paused.

"Will you come inside for a while?" she asked. "I don't think I will be able to sleep now, and I want to know more about you and your father. If you wish to tell me, that is."

Surprised by her invitation—for she had clearly voiced her displeasure when he pushed the limits of propriety the night before—he nodded and followed her into the room.

The bed was in shambles. Clearly she had been tossing and turning as well, and he was unsettled by the extent of pleasure he derived from that observation.

His eyes turned to the fire. It seemed quite dead, but upon closer scrutiny he discovered a few glowing embers of warmth still thriving in the ash.

Anne set her candle down on the bedside table, and Garrett set his own down on the chest of drawers near the hearth.

"Are you still cold?" he asked. "If you like, I can freshen this fire for you."

"That would be wonderful, thank you."

He knelt down and threw a few kindling sticks onto the grate. Within minutes new flames caught and burned. He loaded larger sticks of wood and another log, leaned the iron poker against the marble casing, brushed the dust off his hands, and turned to face Anne.

Her complexion glowed like smooth ivory in the dim firelight, and the beauty of her face stole his breath.

He wondered why he had come in here. More self-inflicted punishment? Or perhaps he craved pleasure, at any cost.

Or something *more* than physical pleasure.

It had been so long since he'd felt that side of his emotions.

"You're still cold," he said, watching her rub at her upper arms and feeling a strong stirring of arousal. "You should go back to bed."

And he should do the proper thing. He should walk to the door and *leave*, but he had spent the better part of the night dreaming about making love to her. He couldn't resist this opportunity to be alone with her.

They weren't playing by the rules anyway. This whole arrangement was outside the normal realm of propriety.

He watched her climb onto the bed and slip beneath the heavy crimson covers.

"I feel guilty," she said.

"Why?" he asked, slowly strolling closer.

"Because I want to continue talking to you about your father, but it's freezing in here. While I am warm in my bed, you are . . ." She paused.

"Suffering miserably in the chill?"

And from a host of other things, too, but he had the grace not to mention them.

Anne watched Garrett approach the bed and knew they were treading into very dangerous territory. He was handsome and virile, full of intriguing mystery, and after their stolen kisses last night, she was finding it more and more difficult to remember the fact that this was supposed to be a charade.

She had been floating in a thick haze of sexual desire all day long, and when she found Garrett wandering the corridors outside her bedchamber a short while ago, she'd wondered if he might have come to steal a few more secret intimacies. She had experienced a thrill like no other and was perversely disappointed to discover he was only searching for a ghost.

But now he was here, in her bedchamber, like a beautiful masculine dream figure, and she didn't want their time together to end.

"I appreciate your concern for my basic comforts," he replied, his voice pleasantly sensual.

As he approached her slowly, he reminded her of a hungry lion, carefully creeping closer so as not to frighten off its prey.

She was completely spellbound. Ready to be devoured. If she had any sense, she would steel herself immediately and suggest that he leave this very instant, but any hope for responsible behavior was fading fast with each step he took closer to the bed.

If only she could forget about the soft touch of his lips the night before. If only she could shut her eyes to the captivating sight of his strong, muscular form.

What would he do if she let him stay? How far would he take this, and more importantly, how far would *she* allow it to go? She didn't want to be the sort of woman who lived up to her notorious reputation, but this was so very difficult.

He reached the bed and paused at the foot of it. "May I join you?"

"Yes," she impulsively replied, than made one last effort to behave somewhat respectably. "But only if you promise to remember that we are not yet married. Can I trust you?"

A lazy grin touched his lips and he squinted at her. "I'm not sure. Should I leave?"

Damn him. Her body was on fire. She could no more tell him to leave than she could stop herself from breathing.

Though she gave no reply, she supposed her expression was enough, for he leisurely moved around the bed and slid under the covers beside her.

Determined to cling to the safe haven of their earlier conversation—which was far less risky than the wild attraction presently firing her blood—Anne rolled to face Garrett and rested her cheek on her palm.

"In the corridor you asked me how much I knew about you and your father, but you revealed nothing after that. Now I am curious to know why the two of you were not close."

Garrett rolled to face her. "Now I feel foolish," he said. "I thought you invited me in here to seduce me."

She should have been unsettled by the suggestion, but instead, she was wickedly aroused.

"Garrett," she whispered. "You promised."

"Did I?" His tone was playful, teasing, enthralling.

"It was implied," she said, "and my curiosity must be satisfied." She struggled to keep the conversation going, not to let her passions take over. "There seem to be many secrets at Pembroke. What happened between you and your father? Why did you leave here all those years ago and not return for seven years?"

He rolled onto his back and stared up at the canopy. The firelight danced on the walls and the flames crackled noisily in the hearth. "I will be blunt, Anne, because you should know the truth. Charlotte and I are not true Sinclairs. Not by blood at least. The duke is not our true father."

Surprised, Anne leaned up on an elbow. "Does he know?"

Garrett turned his head on the pillow to look at her. "Yes. He's always known. I don't know how, exactly. Perhaps Mother simply told him, or he recognized that we looked nothing like him. All I know is that it was never a happy marriage and he despised me quite openly, for I represented all that he could not control. My mother, specifically." Garrett paused and studied Anne's face. She nodded and he continued.

"He treated me like dirt under his boot. If he was not shouting at me or punishing me for something I hadn't done, he was simply ignoring me, treating me as if I were invisible. On the day I left, he had spotted me in the garden with a very highborn young lady with a blood connection to the Queen. He called me inside and told me I should stay away from her, that if one of his sons should have her, it would be Devon. It was the last straw. I told him to go choke on his opinions, and that I would court whomever I damn well pleased. He knocked me around a bit, gave me a bloody lip, but I wasn't a child anymore. I fought back and swung a chair at him."

"Good heavens."

"I swore it would be the last time he would ever raise a hand to me, and it was."

Anne digested all of this. "Were you in love with that girl?"

Garrett shook his head. "No, we were just friends, but it was a matter of principle. I left for Greece the very next day. Father provided me with an allowance under the condition that I stay away, but informed me that upon his death, I would not receive any inheritance. It was no great surprise. I always knew I would never inherit the title, even if something happened to my older brothers. He made that very clear to me early on." Garrett looked at her. "So if you thought you were marrying a man who is fourth in line to a dukedom, that will never be the case."

"I didn't expect to be a duchess," she assured him. "That is not why I accepted this proposal ... but you already knew that." She had been very forthcoming about her motivations to engage in this ruse.

He nodded.

"I suppose," she continued, "you could call me a fortune hunter, in a sense, but not a social climber, at least."

Anne continued to gaze at him in the dim firelight, while her body hummed with physical awareness. "Do you know who your real father is?" she asked.

"No."

"Are you curious about it?"

He breathed deeply. "Sometimes."

All of a sudden, Garrett sat up and leaned on one arm to face her. Instinctively, she lay back on the pillows.

"What you said to me last night," he whispered, changing the subject entirely, "about being an easy conquest . . . I never presumed that about you and I certainly didn't intend to treat you that way."

"I'm surprised to hear that," she replied, feeling defensive, "because that's what everyone *else* presumed when I was surrounded by scandal. People sent me cruel letters. Some were anonymous, other were signed. My father disowned me and called me a whore. But that is not what I am, Garrett, and I will not be defined by my past, nor will I harbor bitterness toward those who wronged me. Instead I will pity them, for they do not know compassion or forgiveness."

He gently stroked her cheek with the pad of his finger. "I am sorry that happened to you."

A brief shiver rippled through her.

"If I was disrespectful last night, I apologize," he added, stroking her hair away from her face.

Anne's breath came short at the pleasure of his touch and his soft breath fanning her face.

But still, she fought to quell her desires, for she did not wish to be a wanton woman that men leered at.

"Yet here you are," she said, "slipping into my bed during the first week of our acquaintance."

His head drew back. "You can trust me. I won't try to make love to you. Not unless you invite me to."

"I am not . . ." She hesitated. "I am *not* inviting you."

For a long moment he gazed into her eyes. Then he nodded. "I understand." .

But he didn't roll away, get out of the bed, make for the door. He continued to lean over her, stroking her cheek, tucking a lock of hair behind her ear.

Pleasantly surprised by this unexpected tenderness, which was more seductive than the most blatant flirtation, she asked, "Why aren't you leaving?"

"Do you want me to?"

"No."

"Then I will stay if you have no objections. We can just talk, or lie here together and not say a word."

She paused, certain it was some kind of trick, because a fiery passion was sizzling between them. She could feel it everywhere—in her heart, her mind, her body.

"Why?"

He shrugged casually, but there was something melancholy in his voice when he spoke. "I don't sleep well. I have unpleasant dreams."

She reached out to lay a hand on his cheek. "Do you dream about the accident?"

He nodded.

The firelight flickered in the room while she ran her fingers through his thick, wavy hair. "Then stay . . . for a while," she said. "I am inviting you to do that, at least."

He gazed down at her for long time. "May I kiss you?" he asked. "Just one kiss."

She should say no. She should not let it go any further, but she wanted to know him more deeply. Just having his body next to hers, quickened her blood. The thought of kissing him was too tempting to resist. No amount of self-restraint was powerful enough to stop her.

"Yes, I'd like that."

She wanted his mouth on hers now, this instant, to feel the intimacy of another soul-reaching kiss. Shamelessly, she reached out to take his face in her hands and pull him closer.

In response, he slid a hand down the side of her body as their lips met and their tongues mingled hotly in the quiet wintry night.

Again, smoldering sensation overwhelmed better judgement. Anne wanted Garrett desperately. She wanted this blissful passion from him.

He devoured her mouth. Her body ached for more, yet her emotions were in tumult. After everything she just said to him about how she would not be defined by her reputation, she was falling under a handsome man's spell yet again, like some light-skirted strumpet.

Then, just when she felt certain she would lose the fight and surrender completely and shamelessly to the storm of passion that was pulsing through her body, Garrett brought the kiss to a smooth, enchanting finish. The kiss continued to linger upon her lips even as he drew away to look down at her.

With her breath held and heart beating fast, she blinked up at him.

"That was nice," he whispered, and she nodded in return.

He relaxed on the bed beside her and gathered her into his arms.

Anne finally exhaled and rested her cheek on his shoulder.

This was not what she had expected when she'd invited him into her room, but it was perfect—all of it—for she'd enjoyed the kiss she had been daydreaming about. Now she was lying beside him, safe and warm in his arms. She let her eyes fall closed and began to relax, even while her body still trembled with desire ...

When she opened her eyes, she was surprised to discover it was morning and the sun was beaming in through the windows.

Anne sat up.

Garrett was gone. He must have left her bed sometime during the night.

He had kept his promise. He had not tried to make love to her. She was relieved to have made it through the night, free of ravishment, but as she rose to get dressed, she realized with a heavy pang of unease that it only made her want him *more*.

How was she ever going to survive until the wedding night?

Chapter Eight

*T*HE ANNUAL CHILDREN'S Christmas concert at the church hall in the village was a cozy affair for the aristocratic ladies of Pembroke Palace, and a very special occasion for Anne, who had not set foot in church since that disheartening day four years ago, when she had been so firmly cast out by the members of her community.

Today, there was only charity and mirth in the air. Evergreen wreaths were hung on the post of every pew, and each family was permitted to take one home to decorate their door. The choral music was both moving and cheerful with the jingle of sleigh bells to accompany the children's voices.

Afterward the ladies enjoyed a light lunch of egg salad sandwiches and fruitcake, and hot mulled cider to drink.

While Anne watched the young mothers with their small children, she envied their conventional lives. She had chosen a very different path—one of personal freedom and financial security—but the events of the past few days had caused her to doubt her decision. She was growing melancholy over the idea that she'd never have a true marriage with a man who was passionately devoted her, heart, body, and soul.

She had not expected to feel such an intense attraction to her betrothed, nor had she expected to mix so comfortably with his sister, his brothers, and their wives.

She raised a cup of cider to her lips and sipped the last few drops while the vicar thanked everyone for attending the concert. He asked that they leave a donation for the less fortunate as they departed.

Anne glanced up with surprise when Charlotte touched her arm. "Are you ready to leave?"

"Yes, I beg your pardon. I was lost in thought."

She joined Charlotte, Rebecca, Chelsea, and the duchess, and together they made their way to the coach. The women waved at the villagers as they drove off.

As soon as they were underway, the duchess clasped Anne's gloved hand. "My dearest Lady Anne," she said, "I hope we have made you feel welcome here at Pembroke."

Anne felt all the other ladies staring at her intently, waiting eagerly for her to reply.

"You have, Your Grace. I cannot thank you enough for your hospitality."

"Please, you must call me Adelaide," the duchess replied. "And we are all so pleased to have you with us, aren't we girls?"

Charlotte, Rebecca, and Chelsea all nodded their heads in enthusiastic agreement.

Anne regarded them with bewilderment. "What is going on? I feel as if you are about to pounce on me with some extraordinary piece of news."

Adelaide squeezed her hand. "We would never pounce, Lady Anne, but I confess we have conspired to speak to you privately today."

A flash of anxiety sparked within her. "Have I done something wrong?"

Did they know? Had the duchess somehow discovered that Anne was having wicked, indecent thoughts about her son ... that she wanted to debauch him?

"Of course not," Adelaide replied. "To the contrary, you have done everything right, Lady Anne. We absolutely adore you. Even the duke cannot stop singing your praises. He thinks you are the most charming creature alive, the last piece of the puzzle that will end the Pembroke Palace curse once and for all."

Anne took the compliment in stride, but it all seemed rather silly, for there really was no curse and they all knew it. The duke was losing his mind, and she was being *paid* to be charming.

"I am pleased to hear it," she said nevertheless.

The coach rumbled through the slush and snow, while Anne continued to sit beside the duchess, facing the other three ladies on the opposite seat. They were all staring at her with bright smiling faces.

"We wish to make you a proposition," Charlotte said at last. "And we hope you will consider it."

Anne regarded them uncertainly. "Another proposition? After the last one your brothers proposed in my uncle's drawing room, I cannot imagine what it might be."

They all laughed graciously as if she were the most witty person on earth, and she wondered if something had been added to the hot cider back at the church hall.

The duchess patted her hand. "It's nothing outrageous, Lady Anne. We simply want you to know that you are welcome to stay at Pembroke Palace as long as you wish. We understand that you signed some sort of document agreeing to leave after the wedding when Garrett returns to Greece, but those terms were drawn up before any of us had a chance to meet you. Devon and Blake quite agree that you fit in well here.

"We feel that if you marry Garrett, you should be treated as a true member of the family. I daresay you will be my beloved daughter-in-law whether or not my son remains in England. We therefore want you to know that we would all be honored and pleased if you were to decide to remain here with us."

Anne couldn't speak for a moment. This was wholly unexpected. "Does Garrett know about this? Has he agreed to it as well?"

Charlotte and the duchess locked gazes. Anne knew immediately that the answer was no.

"We haven't spoken to him about it yet," Charlotte explained. "Mostly because we don't want to put pressure on him. We are quite sure he has not changed his mind about returning to Greece. At least not yet. He says he still wants to remain a bachelor and live elsewhere."

"Which is why it won't make any difference to him whether you stay or go," the duchess added.

Anne cleared her throat. "I will have to consult the terms of the contract, but I believe it stipulates that I, too, will live elsewhere. If I stay, I could be in breach, and therefore would lose the annuity that is promised to me."

The others were quiet.

"Perhaps we could draw up a new contract that allows you more freedom to live where you choose?" Chelsea suggested.

"Garrett would have to sign it," Anne replied, "and I am not comfortable proposing such a thing to him. Please do not misunderstand—I like your son very much, Adelaide. But I do not wish to burden him or put him in an awkward situation should he not wish to change the terms. I really think we should leave everything as it is." She paused, then shook her head. "He does not want a true wife, and I do not wish to try and change his mind."

But why not? she asked herself. Wouldn't it be a dream come true to have him as a husband who would genuinely love her, pleasure her, share a bed with her, be devoted to her?

Of course it would be, but that was nothing but a pipe dream, an existence he did not want, and she certainly didn't come here to put herself in the painful position of getting her heart broken again. She had resolved to be independent and not rely on any man, for she had suffered at the hands of every man she had ever trusted.

She'd already made things more difficult for herself by kissing Garrett and dreaming about him romantically, but she could not rely on him to rescue her.

An uncomfortable silence ensued while the coach wheels sliced through the soft, melting snow.

"But you both seem so well-suited to each other," Charlotte said with disappointment. "I thought perhaps there was a chance you might fall in love, and that he might choose to stay as well."

Anne regarded Charlotte with understanding. "It is clear you love your brother very much," she said. "I cannot blame you. He is a wonderful man, but the truth is ... I cannot pin my hopes on him. He has made it clear to me that he is not seeking a life of matrimony in the conventional sense. Please understand that I must protect myself."

Eventually, the duchess patted her hand. "We understand," she reluctantly said. "But this offer will remain in effect. Once you marry my son, you will always be welcome here, Anne. If you ever want for anything, anything at all, you need only ask."

Anne thanked her and gazed out the window. It was important that she try and forget about their proposition, for it would not be wise to dream about a life—and a love—that was beyond her grasp. Garrett did not want a true marriage and she must honor that.

She felt Charlotte's eyes on her suddenly and pasted on a smile in an effort to appear comfortable with her decision.

Charlotte smiled at her in return, but the rest of the coach ride was filled with light conversations about the weather, while Anne felt completely and utterly exposed.

Chapter Nine

$\mathcal{A}$S SHE DRESSED for dinner that night, Anne hoped she could remain aloof and sensible about Garrett, but even before she walked into the drawing room for drinks, her pulse leapt with excitement at the mere notion that she would see him again.

She began to wonder how much longer she could behave virtuously. This powerful sexual pull was growing stronger each day. Was it even worth the fight? They would be married in a week regardless and would consummate the marriage at that time. What difference would a few days make if they chose to consummate it earlier? Why not steal some pleasure for herself until he left? Lord knows she had gone long enough without. But could she manage it? How would she survive if she fell more deeply in love with him and then he deserted her afterward without a care? As the contract said he would.

When at last he entered the drawing room, her body responded with an explosive round of desire, and she was forced to accept that all her lofty goals to remain aloof had been defeated. She was in love with Garrett. There would be no escaping it.

Tonight he wore formal black dinner attire with a white waistcoat and tie. His golden hair was damp at the ends, as if he had just stepped out of the bath, and that image of him stepping out ... well that alone was enough to upset her whole cart of sensible intentions.

She turned to face the other direction, so that she couldn't stare at him like a love-struck fool.

A moment later, she felt a hand on her arm and knew it was him even before she turned around.

"Good evening," he said.

Just the sound of his voice sent her reeling into a place where the future seemed far less important than the sizzling thrill of the present moment.

Heaven help her, for she knew she would soon be done for ... if given the opportunity.

༄༙༄

After a day spent sleeping late and playing billiards with his brothers—and sipping far too much cognac—Garrett assumed dinner would be a stodgy affair and he would be too drunk to respond to Anne's singular, sensual beauty.

He was proven wrong, however, when he walked into the drawing room and saw her in that form-fitting blue gown, which took on an ethereal glow in the evening light. He got a whiff of lilac perfume as he approached, and had to work hard to remind himself theirs was not a love affair. Not an affair of the heart. There was a binding contract between them. Tonight was a performance for his father's benefit, nothing more.

"Good evening." Her smile was luminous. "I heard you were engaged in a billiards game today, and that it lasted many hours."

"That's right," he replied. "And I heard you attended a children's concert in the village that melted everyone's hearts."

Her full lips curled into a mischievous grin and her eyes twinkled. "The children were quite adorable."

She was adorable. Impossibly beautiful. Utterly irresistible. *And no child.*

A footman came by with two crystal glasses of sherry on a silver tray. Garrett picked them up and handed Anne one.

"I wasn't sure if you would be angry with me today," he softly said, glancing over his shoulder to ensure no one was listening.

"Why would I be angry?" she asked.

He paused. "Sometimes a woman is displeased when a gentleman leaves her bed in the night without saying good-bye."

Anne slowly sipped on her drink. "A woman would only be displeased if the gentleman had taken improper liberties with her, but you were a perfect gentleman last night, Garrett. So no, I am not angry. But I am curious. How long did you stay?"

He glanced over his shoulder again. "Most of the night. I left just before dawn."

"Did you sleep at all?"

"Very well, in fact."

"No unpleasant dreams?"

"Not a single one. I should thank you for that."

His shoulders relaxed, but the agitation did not leave him, for he still wanted to bed her in the worst, most ungentlemanly way.

"If you like, you could come again tonight," she quietly suggested, running the tip of her finger around the rim of her glass.

Was it possible her resolve was weakening? Garrett wondered as he tried to decipher her motives and her intent.

"Are you sure that would be wise?" he asked.

"Why wouldn't it be?"

He glanced around. "What would the others say if they knew?"

Her eyes glimmered like gemstones, and the ring on her finger flashed brilliantly in the firelight. "I don't think that is your chief concern," she said.

"No?" he asked.

One dark, arched eyebrow rose a fraction. "No. I think you are terrified you might fall in love with me, Garrett, then all your ambitious plans for a life of loneliness and despair would be undone. That would be terribly disappointing, would it not?"

The butler entered just then to announce that dinner was served.

Surprised and more than a little disconcerted by Anne's daring inference, he offered his arm and escorted her into the dining room.

Later, when dessert was served, he leaned close to her ear and told her in no uncertain terms that he was afraid of nothing.

Then he told her exactly what time he would arrive at her bedchamber door that evening, and suggested she be ready for him.

ᘒᘓᘔ

With a mischievous note of challenge, Anne rolled to face Garrett on the bed and propped her cheek on a hand. "I suppose you've been with a lot of women?"

"A few," he casually replied, sweeping her hair away from her face so he would not lose sight of her bewitching beauty. "Is there something you wish to know?"

She began to run her fingers lightly over his chest—a rather flirtatious manoeuvre which again surprised him. He let his eyes fall closed and settled in to enjoy the heavenly splendor of her touch.

"I am curious about something, actually," she said.

"What is it?"

She continued to tease him with light, featherlike strokes. "Is there someone else waiting for you? Someone you could not marry for some reason? Is that why you wanted a binding contract to ensure your freedom? So that you could leave here immediately after the wedding?"

He found himself wondering how much it mattered to her. If he said yes, would she stop running her fingers across his chest and freeze over with jealousy? Or would she tell him it did not matter, for this was merely a business arrangement?

He opened his eyes and watched her expression carefully. "There is no one else."

"But there must have been ... *once*."

He hesitated to speak of it, or even think about it, but did not wish to keep anything from her, for she had been very open with him thus far.

"Yes, there was someone."

Her expression remained unchanged. "I see."

Clearly, she was working hard to keep her feelings hidden from him.

And what were her feelings, exactly? Was she dreaming of something more between them? Was this a sign of her growing affection? Or was it possessiveness?

Jealousy and emotional turmoil were not things he'd wanted from this charade, for he had been trapped once before.

But no ... not Anne ... *please*. He did not want her to have such a plan in her mind.

"You wish to know more," he cautiously said. "You want to know why I left it to my brothers to find me a bride."

Strangely, despite everything, he wanted to tell her.

"I admit I am curious."

He wrapped an arm about her shoulders and pulled her close, wondering if it would be a mistake to continue this conversation. Surely it was too intimate. It would reveal too much.

At the same time it seemed rather selfish of him to tell her the truth, as if it would somehow ease his guilt, release his shame into the world and lighten his own heart—when he, and he alone, deserved to live with it for the rest of his days.

"Remember when I told you I lost my boat?" he said, because it was too late to turn back now. "I lied when I said I was alone. There were others with me. A woman I intended to marry and her nephew—the son of her brother and his wife, who were also on board."

Anne sat up. "You were engaged?"

He nodded.

"What happened to her? Was she lost with the boat?"

He nodded again, and she stared back at him in shock.

"Good heavens." Anne stared at him speechless, as if she had no notion what to say. "What caused the boat to sink?" she asked. "You never really told me about it."

He exhaled heavily. "A sudden squall came out of nowhere and turned the boat over. I tried to save everyone, but somehow, for some reason I will never understand, I was the only survivor."

"Oh, Garrett," she replied. "I had no idea. You haven't told anyone in your family?"

"No."

All at once, he wanted to rise from the bed and walk out. Leave the house and go straight back to Greece to be alone, where no one asked any questions, but he forced himself to remain beside her.

"When did this happen?"

"In the spring."

Anne cleared her throat. "Why did you only come home now, and why do you want the money? Do you wish to buy a new boat?"

"No. I mean to give the money to Georgina's parents. They lost a great deal that day."

Anne sat in silence, digesting all of this, then turned her face away. "I cannot believe you were engaged, and that she died. I'm so sorry."

She'd turned away, as he thought she might. He really didn't want to go on talking about this. It was exhausting.

Anne faced him again and laid a hand on his cheek. "If it was an unexpected squall, it couldn't have been your fault. I'm sure you did everything you could to prevent the worst from happening."

He removed her hand from his face and set it away from him. "I've gone over every detail and there were a dozen things I could have done differently that might have changed the outcome. I could have stayed in bed that day, for one. I could have turned the boat around after dinner instead of staying out to watch the sunset. Or I could have drowned with the others instead of saving myself by grabbing hold of the life ring."

He saw the frown in her eyes and wondered if she would change her mind about marrying him. He wouldn't blame her if she did.

"Everyone else was down below," he explained, "trying to stay dry. "I was the only one up on deck. When the boat flipped over, they were trapped inside. I tried to help them when we were going down, but I couldn't get to them."

Except for the boy. Johnny. He had held onto his hand for as long as he could ...

Garrett suddenly wished he hadn't come here tonight. He'd wanted to escape the accident, not revisit it. Was it too much to ask to spend a few blissful hours in the arms of an angel?

"I think you should tell your family," Anne said. "They should know."

He shook his head. "I just want to leave it be. I shouldn't have told you. I don't know why I did."

He slid across the bed and reached for his robe, pulled it on and stood up.

"Wait, don't go." Anne climbed out the other side and rushed around the foot of the bed to meet him. She took hold of his hands. "We don't have to talk about that, and I promise I won't say anything to anyone. Please, just stay."

Her arms slid around his waist. She stepped into his embrace and rested her cheek on his chest.

Not a good idea, yet he found himself cupping the back of her head and holding her tight against him. He could feel the lush pressure of her breasts; her hair was like silk.

Desire burned through him and then the last thing he wanted to do, was talk. Or leave. He wanted only to hold her, taste her, satisfy this raging sexual arousal that had been plaguing him since the first moment he saw her.

Before he could think to resist, he pressed his mouth to hers and kissed her deeply as he lifted her onto the bed.

His angel lay back before him. She blinked up at him with desire while he ripped off his robe and tossed it to the floor.

"If you don't want me to make love to you," he said, "you must tell me now."

She inched across the mattress to make room for him. "We'll be married anyway. I'm tired of fighting this."

"Is that a yes?"

She hesitated. "I think so."

Garrett's eyes narrowed while he paused at the edge of the bed. "I need a firmer answer than that, Anne. Otherwise, I should leave."

Seconds of painful, agonizing anticipation ticked by while she considered it. "I'm ... *nervous*."

Garrett quickly reined in his passions. He took a few deep, calming breaths. "We won't do anything you don't want to do. I'll stop if you ask me to. At any time, I promise. I just want to be with you."

Anne gazed up at him with uncertainty.

❦

There it was ... His need for her was more than sexual.

Anne swallowed uneasily while her mind whirled in confusion. She wanted him with mad fury, wanted to feel his hands on her body, wanted to give herself over to him completely.

But why? Was it purely wanton lust, or was it something more? He was obviously tormented by guilt and needed an escape. She understood that.

He needed pleasure to help him forget, and she wanted to be there for him.

But no, no, she was not that altruistic. As she watched his chest heave with barely controlled desire, she knew that, above all, this was lust. Dirty, greedy, hungry lust.

Responding to a wild flash of yearning, she rose up on her knees and began to tug at his nightshirt, lifted it over his head, tossed it onto the floor.

He now stood naked before her in the warm, golden glow of the firelight, and she stared at him with longing.

"You have your answer," she said, admiring his smooth muscled chest, running her hands over his arms and shoulders, down to his slender torso and hips. "I want you to stay."

His mouth covered hers in a violent kiss of unrestrained passion. Then he came down upon her—his hand cradling her head, his nude body gloriously hot and heavy, pulsing against her, pressing her into the mattress.

She let out a tiny, breathless moan as he unbuttoned the collar of her nightdress and kissed the tops of her breasts. Their mouths collided in another violent surge of hunger and desire as he tugged roughly at her hem to gain better access to her thighs and hips and all the magic in between.

"Take this off." His voice was low and fierce.

Anne sat up and removed her nightgown. As she sat naked before him, the peaks of her breasts firm and alert, she was aroused beyond any dream or fantasy, and wanted—no, she *needed*—to feel him inside her now ... *Now*. She couldn't wait any longer.

His lips found hers again and he kissed her, more gently this time, slowing the frantic, ragged pace upon which they had begun.

"Lie back," he commanded, and she readily obeyed.

He leaned up on elbow beside her and ran the pad of his thumb across her nipples, then slid his palm smoothly down the center of her flat, quivering belly to the juncture between her thighs.

She was aching with need by this time and the wet fire between her thighs was tingling, begging to be explored. His hand slid into the damp folds, stroked her for a moment or two before he slipped his middle finger inside.

Anne arched her back and groaned as orgasmic sensation flooded her body. It was too soon. They'd only just begun, but her mind had been filled with sexual visions for days now, and she simply couldn't hold back. He thrust his finger in and out of her a few times until she cried out, stiffened and convulsed with searing, trembling pleasure.

He continued to slide his hand around, pleasuring her until the climax eased off and her body relaxed to the smooth thrusting sensations. She opened her eyes and looked at him, worried that she had behaved too wantonly, but he was gazing at her with fascination.

"Anne ..." He rolled on top of her.

She spread her legs wide, wrapped them around his hips and lifted her head off the pillow to meet his kiss. She felt him down below—the firm but velvety tip of his erection pushing against the entrance to her womanhood. His skin was warm against her breasts. She couldn't seem to get close enough. She wanted more, to hold him tighter. Oh, how she reveled in the pleasure of his mouth kissing the side of her neck. His tongue darted out to probe into the hollow beneath her collarbone. It was all so dreamlike.

He slid into her then, and she cried out at the overwhelming invasion of his body into hers. He filled her completely. She could barely breathe.

"Are you all right?" he asked, moving slowly within.

She answered him with a nod and a kiss as she pushed her hips upward to meet each of his deep rhythmic thrusts. He moved carefully at first, as if he were fighting against some primitive need to push into her like a beast, then gave in to his impulses and made love to her with deep penetrations that took her breath away.

He braced both hands on the bed on either side of her, arched his back and shut his eyes as if in tortuous pain. Then he shot his seed into her with a spectacular throbbing, drenching rush of heat and wetness.

Anne wrapped her arms around him as he collapsed on top of her. She couldn't seem to hold him close enough or tight enough. Her heart was racing. She hadn't known it could feel like this. She felt both astounded and awakened. How was this possible? And what was she going to do?

She had only one more week with him. Then what? Would she be able to accept the loss of him?

She could not bear to imagine her world without him. Without *this*.

Chapter Ten

A LIGHT SNOW FELL during the night, but by morning the family woke to milder temperatures, a clear blue sky, and the sound of water dripping from the eaves. By late afternoon, however, the temperature dropped as quickly as it had risen, and all the puddles turned to ice.

Garrett lay alone in his bed, staring up at the canopy, recalling all the sensual pleasures he'd enjoyed in Anne's bed the night before, and wondering if she would be agreeable to more of the same this evening.

Again, he had slept all night with her. There were no dreams of stormy seas and drowning faces. Only peace and ... well, exhaustion.

He was about to get up and visit Anne in her bedchamber for a brief time before tea when a knock sounded at his door.

"Come in," he said as he swung his booted feet to the floor.

A footman burst in to the room. "My lord. Her Grace is asking for you. She is in the duke's chamber. She said to hurry."

Garrett flew off the bed and followed the footman.

A moment later he was striding into his father's chamber where his mother was pacing back and forth in front of the window.

"Garrett, I'm so glad you are here. We cannot locate your father. Dr. Thomas is scheduled to arrive at any moment for their regular appointment, but now your father is missing."

"Did he not want to be examined today?" Garrett asked.

"He never wants to be examined. I told him to stay in bed, but when I returned he was gone. The servants have searched all the rooms, but we haven't been able to find him."

Garrett strode to the window, pulled the curtain aside with one finger and scanned the courtyard and snow-covered lawns in the distance. "What was he wearing? Did he take a topcoat?"

"No, he was dressed only in his nightshirt. He is not wearing shoes."

Garrett faced his mother. "Where are Devon and Blake? Have you told them?"

"They have already left for London with Chelsea and Rebecca to see the solicitor and banker about the will. They won't be back until late tomorrow. I don't know what to do. Where could he be?"

"Don't worry, we'll find him." Garrett glanced around the room for signs of something—anything—out of order. "Was he distraught when you left him?"

"No more than usual."

"And you've searched all the rooms?"

She nodded. "The servants are still looking everywhere. Perhaps we should send a search party outside. What if he went to the lake house? It's been sunny and mild the past few days. The ice isn't safe."

Garrett hurried to the door and called the footman. "You there, come here at once. Go out to the stables and tell the grooms to take a few horses to the lake. We must find the duke."

"Yes, my lord."

Garrett swung around to face his mother. Her brow was creased with concern. "Was he talking about the ghosts again?"

"Not that I know of. He just seemed frightened and restless."

"Has anyone checked the chapel? Could he have gone down to the tunnels?"

She sucked in a breath. "Possibly. I didn't think of that. Why didn't I?"

He squeezed her hand and moved quickly to the door. "I will go and search there. In the meantime inform Lady

Anne about what is happening. She is a good person to help search. She has a calming effect on him."

ᘒᘓᘔ

Just as Garrett had suspected, the chapel door was wide open, the loose stone that concealed the key was dislodged, the key was missing, and the door to the catacombs was ajar.

He had come prepared with a lantern and blanket, and was about to duck his head low to pass through the small door when he heard rapid footsteps on the flagstones outside. Turning to look, he breathed a sigh of relief when he saw Anne, dressed in a warm cloak, rushing up the chapel steps. She, too, had come with a lantern. He could have kissed her.

"There you are," she said, out of breath. "Your mother told me you came here to search."

"Yes." He waved her over. "I see you brought another lantern. Good thinking. Perhaps we can split up this time. You can go left, and I will go right."

"That is precisely what I was thinking."

Together they ducked through the entrance and descended the steep steps to the underground level where the air was cold and damp. Holding Anne's hand, Garrett led the way to the end of the first long corridor. When they reached the T, Garrett turned to her. "If you find him, shout as loud as you can and I will come to you. I will do the same. Otherwise, I will meet you back in the chapel. If you do not return within an hour I will send another search party after you."

"But what if your father has escaped out the other door? If he has done so, I will follow his footsteps in the snow."

"Yes," Garrett replied. "I will do the same. We must each leave that door open to signal that we have left the passages to pursue him."

With a steady nod, she disappeared into the left vein. Garrett hurried to the right, grateful for Anne's clear head and helpful presence.

Chapter Eleven

"*F*ATHER!" GARRETT SHOUTED as he rounded another curve. A mouse scurried along the wall at his feet. "Are you here?"

He had been calling out to the duke since he entered the catacombs, and could hear the faint sound of Anne doing the same, but there had been no replies.

The passageway narrowed before him and he held the lantern aloft to slip sideways through the tight space.

He stopped when he heard a moan up ahead, like that of a child. *A boy.* All the hairs on the back of his neck stood on end. For a moment he could not move.

"Who's there?" he called out. "Where are you?"

Garrett's insides flooded with sickening dread as recurrent images of that frightful day on the water came crashing into his brain. *The wind in the sails, the stinging spray in his face, the thunderous sound of the water filling his ears . . .*

Garrett shut his eyes and strove to control his breathing. This was not Johnny, returned from the dead to haunt him. There were no ghosts here, only guilt and regret.

"*Where am I?*"

Garrett's eyes flew open as he recognized the sound of his father's voice. His turned in that direction.

"Father! You are in the tunnel network beneath the chapel." He moved faster through the narrow passageway until he reached the duke, who was frozen with fear, trapped against the wall, dressed only in a white nightshirt.

"It's me, Garrett. Are you all right?" Then he called out to Anne. "I've found him! We are over here!"

The duke's lips were blue. His teeth chattered and he shivered uncontrollably. "I'm cold. How did I get here?"

Garrett glanced down at his father's bare feet. "Do you not have a candle or a lamp?"

The duke shook his head.

"How in the world did you reach this place in the dark?"

"I don't know," the duke answered. "Where am I?"

"You're in the tunnels beneath the chapel," Garrett repeated. "But do not be concerned. Everything's going to be fine. I'm going to get you out of here and take you home."

"I'm c ... cold," he said.

"I have a blanket for you, but first we must get out of this space."

It was too tight and narrow for Garrett to wrap the blanket around him.

"Which way?" the duke asked.

"Go forward, to your right. Only a few more feet and the corridor will widen."

"But I'm frightened. I don't want to die. Not here."

Garrett spoke in a calm, reassuring voice. "Everything's going to be fine, Father. I am here beside you and I won't leave you, I promise. All you have to do is take a few steps to the right. Can you do that?"

The duke nodded and managed to move shakily along the wall until the corridor opened up again. Garrett pushed his way out and immediately set the lamp down on the ground to wrap the heavy woolen blanket around his father's shoulders.

"Good God, you're freezing," he said, taking him into his arms and rubbing his back. "We need to get you warm again."

The duke inhaled a few shuddering breaths while Garrett felt the alarmingly thin, boney structure of his father's spine and shoulder blades. He was so frail compared to how Garrett remembered him. In his younger days, he had been a large and powerful man who knew how to punish and terrorize—could do it with just a single cold, scathing look down the intimidating length of his nose.

"I c...can't feel my f...feet," the duke said.

Garrett looked down. His father was standing in a puddle of water.

"Take hold of my shoulders," he said. "I will carry you on my back to another door where we will meet Lady Anne. Do you remember her?"

Leaving the lantern on the ground, he bent forward, lifted his father up, and started walking.

"Is she pretty?"

"Yes, she's very pretty," Garrett replied. "She has green eyes and dark hair."

"Is she your wife?"

"Not yet, but she will be soon. We will be married on Christmas Eve." His father clung tightly to Garrett's neck. "We're almost there, Father. Look, see? Here we are."

He reached the rough-hewn wooden steps and set his father down. "Stay here, don't move." He hurried back to fetch the lantern and returned, sat down, and removed his own boots and stockings. "Put these on." He handed his stockings to his father. "They will warm your feet."

With shaking hands, the duke pulled them on and gathered the blanket more tightly about his shoulders while Garrett pulled his boots back on. He was going to need them himself to get his father out of here.

"It's cold," the duke said, still shivering. "What is this place?"

"We're in an old set of tunnels beneath the palace. They were dug out long before you and I were born. Do you remember coming here before?"

He knew for a fact that his father was well acquainted with the catacombs. It was he who had first introduced Garrett and his brothers to the secret door in the chapel when they were children.

"No," he replied, shaking more violently now.

Garrett slid closer and wrapped his arms around him again. "Anne will be here soon. She knows a way to avoid that narrow section. I'm going to call out to her now."

His father nodded.

Garrett shouted as loud as he could. "Anne! I found him! Are you there?"

Like an echo, she replied. "I am almost there!"

Soon, a bright yellow glow illuminated the passageway to the right and he heard the sound of her rapid footsteps splashing through puddles.

When she appeared and stopped breathless before them, he met her gaze with concern.

"He's freezing," Garrett said. "We must get him back to the palace. Can you take both lanterns?"

"Of course. Follow me."

Garrett stood and scooped his father up again, this time in his arms, not on his back. They moved through one dark corridor after another.

"Are you sure it's this way?" Garrett asked as they took a sharp left turn.

"I am positive," she replied.

His father hugged him tightly around the neck. "I'm tired," he said. His head nodded forward.

Garrett was an experienced yachtsman. He knew enough about the effects of the cold upon the human body. His father was seventy-six years old. He should not fall asleep.

"You must stay awake," Garrett commanded, roughly jostling his father about in his arms to startle him. "Can you sing a song for me?" Garrett began to sing *I Heard the Bells on Christmas Day*, and Anne quickly joined in.

"Come along, Your Grace. You're not singing."

The duke began to softly mumble a few bars while Garrett walked faster through the tunnels. The muscles in his arms were burning and his heart was pounding heavily from the exertion, but he pressed on, following Anne through the twisting corridors.

When at last they reached the chapel steps and he looked up at the brightly lit door at the top, he said to her, "Go on ahead of us. Tell Mother we found him, and that we need Dr. Thomas to meet us in the chapel right away."

"He's lost consciousness," she observed.

"Yes." Garrett gently set his father down on the bottom step. "Go now, and hurry."

She carried both lanterns up the steps and disappeared into the chapel.

Garrett gently slapped his father's cheeks. "Father, wake up. Can you hear me?"

The duke's eyes fluttered open, but he gave no reply. His head nodded forward again.

"*Dammit!*" Garrett shouted. He shook his father roughly. "Stay awake!"

Realizing this was hopeless, and he could not wait for assistance, he scooped the duke up into his arms again and carried him up the stairs.

He did not stop when he passed through the door and emerged into the bright rays of colored light streaming in through the stained glass window. With swift, long strides he moved beyond the altar and down the center aisle past the choir stalls.

Anne had left the chapel doors ajar. He kicked them open and passed through to the outdoor courtyard within the cloister, and was blinded by brilliant sunlight upon the white snow. Still, he ran.

He burst through the palace doors and saw Anne and his mother running toward him with Dr. Thomas by her side.

Suddenly mindful of his muscles straining painfully, and fearing that his knees were going to give out beneath him, Garrett stopped and knelt down in the center of the great hall.

Dr. Thomas ran toward him. The look on his face, the expression, was familiar—so like his sister's. As the scene unfolded in slow motion before Garrett's eyes, he was strangely unnerved by it.

The doctor was there in an instant, taking the duke out of his arms. "Good work," he said. "How long has he been unconscious?"

"Only a few minutes," Garrett replied, struggling to catch his breath as he entrusted his father into the doctor's capable hands.

"We must get him upstairs," Dr. Thomas said. "Send for hot water, extra blankets, and warm tea. We'll need to get a strong fire going as well."

Garrett remained there overwhelmed by exhaustion, but even more by possibilities ... possibilities that could explain so much.

Anne laid her hand on his shoulder. "Are you all right?"

He nodded, then staggered to his feet to follow the doctor up the main staircase.

ᖴᘓᘉᖴ

As Garrett sat at his father's bedside clasping his hand, he couldn't help but wonder why he was here at all, caring for the man who had always treated him like the unwanted bastard son that he was.

Nothing had seemed quite the same since his return. The duke was no longer the harsh and cold disciplinarian who ruled this house with an iron fist. Over the past few years, his mind had deteriorated and his body had shriveled. He was now a helpless old man who was terrified of being alone. Of dying.

Garrett understood that fear very well. He had seen it in the eyes of others.

The duke stirred and moaned. "Where am I?"

"You're safe in your bed, Father," Garrett replied. "How are you feeling?"

"Tired."

"Would you like some tea?"

The duke turned his stricken eyes to Garrett. "Who are you?"

The question was like a knife in his heart. They had come so far, or at least he'd thought they had. "I'm Garrett. Your son." The words tasted bitter on his tongue.

Those empty eyes filled with moisture, and the duke's brow furrowed with misery. "Oh, my dear son." He clasped Garrett's hand. "I am so glad you have come home to us at last."

Feeling quite sure that his father did not remember that he was not his true son—but grateful nonetheless that there was love in his eyes—Garrett dropped his gaze and contemplated the situation.

For many years he had convinced himself he was indifferent to his father's emotional neglect, and his cruelty, yet in this moment he could not deny a crippling need to hear a loving word from this man.

"So am I," he replied, his heart fracturing just a little inside, while at the same time, that old animosity simmered beneath it all. All his father had to do was utter a single word of kindness, and all was forgiven?

But Garrett needed kindness now. He needed to know he had some worth. And to hear it from this man, of all people.

His father reached out with a trembling hand and cupped Garrett's cheek. "You're a good boy. I think I was too hard on you." His eyes filled with fear while he struggled to remember. "Was I?"

Garrett swallowed over the emotion rising up within him. "Sometimes ... yes."

A look of regret flashed across his father's face. Then he lowered his hand and blinked up at the canopy. Garrett leaned back.

"Brother Salvador said there is a reason you are still with us," the duke said. "A reason you were not lost."

Garrett looked up. "I beg your pardon?"

"You're not meant to leave yet." The duke rolled over onto to his side and closed his eyes.

Garrett frowned in bewilderment. Did the duke know that he meant to return to Greece immediately after the wedding? Or was he referring to something else?

Something about the accident? Could he know? If so, how?

Garrett pulled the covers up over his father's shoulders and tucked him in as he drifted off to sleep.

A short while later, Dr. Thomas walked in. "How is the patient?" he quietly asked.

"He seems better," Garrett replied.

The doctor laid the back of his hand on the duke's forehead. "His temperature seems normal. I believe he is going to be fine."

"Thank you for everything," Garrett replied. "Especially for taking him out of my arms in the hall. I couldn't have carried him much further."

Dr. Thomas listened to the duke's heart with a scope on his back while consulting his timepiece. "Well. He might have died if you hadn't found him when you did. He's a lucky man to have such a devoted son."

Garrett leaned back in his chair and studied the doctor for a long moment. "Thank you, but I do not feel I can accept the compliment, for I've been absent for the past seven years. I've been sailing around the Mediterranean while my brothers have remained here for the most part, steadfast in their duties."

The doctor glanced up. "I'm sure you had your reasons. You're young. Sometimes it's necessary to fly the coop and expand your horizons. Learn about the world. It all becomes a part of your life experience and later those experiences shape your future." He put his scope back into his medical bag.

Garrett watched him with growing interest. "How long have you been a medical man, if you don't mind my asking?"

"Quite a long time. Since before *you* were born."

"Did you always know you wanted to be a man of science?"

The doctor sat down in the chair on the opposite side of the bed. "Most of my life, yes, though my father wanted me to join the army or navy. He felt it was beneath me to enter the medical profession."

"Who is your father?" Garrett asked, realizing he knew very little about Dr. Thomas.

"Viscount Bradley. He's dead now. My elder brother inherited the title, so at least now I am permitted back home to visit."

Garrett's eyebrows lifted. "Your father cut you off?"

"Yes, when I didn't do what he wanted. He cut me out of his will entirely and we never spoke again." Those familiar eyes met Garrett's. "Which is why you have done the right thing by coming home. I will always wonder if perhaps my own estrangement with my father could have been resolved if I had made the effort. I would sleep better now if it had been."

Garrett considered all this. "If you could go back, would you do things differently and join the army instead? Do you regret your choices?"

Dr. Thomas lowered his gaze. "Certain choices, yes, but not that one. I was never cut out for war. I have no desire to be anywhere near flying bullets—sent or received."

Garrett chuckled. "I cannot blame you. And I envy your ability to restore health to someone who is sick or dying."

They sat in silence for a while.

"What will you do with yourself, Lord Garrett, when you have your inheritance? I understand you will receive a settlement on your wedding day. The duchess tells me you plan to return to Greece."

Garrett sighed. "That was my intention when I returned home, but now I find I am not as eager to leave as I thought I would be."

"I am sure your mother would be pleased to hear that. She's missed you."

Garrett met the doctor's steady gaze and found himself growing more curious about this man by the minute. "How long have you known my mother?"

"A long time."

Garrett paused. "Are you married? Do you have children?"

He cleared his throat. "Sadly I was never fortunate enough to become a husband, which has been my own loss in this life, to be sure. Lady Anne is lovely," he added. "You are a very lucky man."

Garrett thanked the doctor for his assistance, then excused himself from his company—for after talking to Dr. Thomas and again, sensing something disconcertingly familiar in him, Garrett had a question of the utmost importance to ask his mother.

ᛒᚳᚳᛈ

"I agree he is an excellent physician," Adelaide said as she poured Garrett a cup of tea. "Much better than the one who came before him. That useless man refused to recognize that anything was wrong. He said only what your father wanted him to say."

"I'm not surprised," Garrett replied. "Father was always a very intimidating man." He leaned forward and set the cup and saucer down on the table. "There is another reason I am here, however. I have a question about Dr. Thomas."

Without meeting his gaze, Adelaide stirred her own tea and set the tiny spoon down in the saucer with a delicate *clink*.

"How long have you known him?" Garrett asked.

She rose from her chair and walked to the window where she briefly looked out, then turned to face Garrett. "A long time."

Somehow he could sense she knew what he had come here to ask, and that a secret was about to unfold itself.

"What do you want to know, exactly?" she asked.

"Everything. I want to know why Charlotte and I are ..." He paused and took a breath. "I want to know what happened all those years ago. Most of all, I want to know if my suspicions are correct."

Adelaide cleared her throat. "Tell me Garrett. What are your suspicions?"

He went to join her at the window. "When I saw Dr. Thomas walk toward me in the courtyard, it reminded me of Charlotte who ran out to meet me as I arrived home. Some expressions . . . His eyes are so like hers. And mine.

"Mother." Garrett paused and looked directly into her eyes. "Is the man who is caring for your husband at this very moment my *real* father? Or am I the second person in this house to go mad this Christmas?"

Chapter Twelve

ANNE TURNED TO look at her reflection in the cheval glass and glanced uneasily at Charlotte. "It's beautiful, but are you sure you do not mind?"

Charlotte smiled, but there was moisture in her eyes as she fastened the pearl buttons at the back of the gown, a gown designed for her own wedding day. Charlotte had confessed to Anne the night before that her fiancé—the great love of her life—had died tragically before they were married.

"I am sure," she replied. "Look, it fits you perfectly, and someone needs to wear it so it doesn't simply collect dust for the next dozen years."

"Perhaps you might wish to wear it yourself one day?" Anne suggested.

Charlotte shook her head somberly. "No. If I ever marry, I will want a different dress."

While Charlotte worked on the buttons, Anne continued to study her reflection and felt strangely as if she were watching herself move through a dream. One month ago she would never have believed she would be fitted for a wedding gown today.

It was all a charade, of course, and very soon she would begin a new life that did not involve Garrett at all.

"You look stunning," Charlotte said as she fastened the last button. "Now you need jewelry ... Pearls, I think. Yes, that's what this needs." She crossed to her dressing table and withdrew a blue velvet box from the bottom drawer. "These will do perfectly." She returned to close the clasp around Anne's neck.

Anne couldn't find words to describe her emotions. Everything was so perfect. *Now.* "You are too kind, Charlotte. Honestly ..."

Charlotte grinned conspiratorially. "Mark my words, he will fall over backwards when he sees you in the chapel. He won't want to leave. He'll be yours forever."

Anne gathered the heavy silk skirt in her hands and turned away from the cheval glass to face Charlotte. "That is very romantic, but you mustn't say such things. You know the situation." She picked up the train and walked to the chair to sit down.

"I do, but I also know a perfect match when I see one, and I truly believe you and my brother are destined to be together. Why else would all this be happening?"

Anne looked down and ran a finger over the fine silk bodice—an excuse not to look Charlotte in the eye. "I would prefer not to entertain such hopes. I have signed an agreement and I mean to fulfill my obligations."

Charlotte sat down, too. "Entertain such hopes? So you *are* hopeful. You *do* care for him? Please tell me. I consider you my friend. I want to know what you are feeling."

Oh, God . . . Anne kicked herself sternly. She should have chosen her words more carefully. Yet at the same time she feared she might burst if she didn't soon confess her feelings to someone.

"Yes, I do care for him," she said, "but like you, I've had my heart broken. Garrett has been clear on the matter. He does not wish to be a married man. He wants his freedom and does not want a partner in life."

"But if he *did* want that, would you accept him?"

"He doesn't."

"But if he *did*," she pressed. "If he declared himself madly in love with you and told you he couldn't live another day without you, and got down on both knees to beg you to stay and be his true wife, would you not be the happiest woman alive?"

A tiny ember of hope sparked within her at the prospect, and she felt her lips curl into a smile. "I think I would die of happiness," she confessed.

Charlotte's whole face lit up like a sky full of exploding fireworks. "I knew it," she said with a grin.

Anne did not feel quite so jubilant, however, for it was not a dream she dared believe in. She had been disappointed once before by a man who abandoned her for money, and after the scandal, she'd had no choice but to forsake the idea of an honest marriage for herself.

And Garrett—having just tragically lost a fiancée—seemed so very unattainable.

"Please, Charlotte," she said, "Do not encourage me in this. I do not wish to pursue something I cannot have."

"You don't know that."

"No, but I know what I feel, and I fear I am headed for disaster if I imagine a fairy tale ending. I am afraid to believe it. Promise me you will help me keep a clear head."

Charlotte regarded her with reluctance.

"*Promise* me," Anne insisted, "or I will take this gown off immediately and wear the old rag I was wearing when I arrived."

Charlotte drew back in horror. "Good heavens, we cannot have that."

"No, we certainly cannot." Anne lifted the hem and looked down at her stockinged feet. "I will need shoes to go with this. And gloves. Can you help?"

"Of course." Charlotte went to hunt through her wardrobe, while Anne exhaled heavily with a growing angst that was beginning to weigh very heavily upon her heart.

⚜

Garrett followed his mother back to the sofa and urged her to sit down, for she had gone white as a sheet.

"It's been a very trying day," she said. "First your father disappears, now this question from you."

"I only want to know the truth. I already know I am not legitimate, but we have never talked openly about it. Now that I am home, I need to understand."

She clasped his hand. "Of course you do, and I do not wish to keep anything from you. What would be the point now that your father is so ill? He will never come back to us like he once was."

Her voice trembled and Garrett squeezed her hand. "Tell me what happened all those years ago."

His mother sat back in her chair. "I will come straight to the point. Your intuition is correct ... about Dr. Thomas."

For a long moment Garrett said nothing.

"Does Charlotte know?"

Adelaide nodded. "Yes. Like you, she suspected the truth when she met him. He has been coming to the palace since the spring, not long after Devon returned from America. Dr. Thomas is the most brilliant physician in London, and we all wanted the very best for your father."

"Why didn't Charlotte tell me?" Garrett was surprised by this, for she was his twin—but he supposed he deserved to be kept outside the circle. He had abandoned her and the rest of his family by choice.

"She would have told you eventually, I'm sure ... when the time was right."

Garrett massaged his temples and tried to absorb all of this. "Is he your lover?"

"Good heavens, no," he mother firmly replied. "He is a friend to me now. Nothing more."

Garrett frowned. "Does he know I am his son?"

"Yes."

Garrett recalled the moment he dropped to his knees in the Great Hall and Dr. Thomas arrived and took the duke from his arms, and then continued to carry him upstairs. In his mind, Garrett also went over their conversation a short while ago.

Garrett admired the man's intelligence and kindness, but this was not easy to accept.

"It's important for you to know something," Adelaide said. "What happened between Dr. Thomas and me was not a brief, torrid affair. I was very young, to be sure, but I loved him and I still love him, though now it is a quieter sort of love." She stood up and held out her hand. "Let us go for a walk outside in the fresh winter air. If I am going to tell you everything, Garrett, I must start at the beginning."

He took hold of her hand and rose to his feet.

༺ঙঙঙ༻

A short while before it was time to dress for dinner, Anne was resting in her bed, fighting to clear her mind of Garrett, when a knock sounded at her door.

She rose to answer it and found herself staring at the very face she was working so hard to forget.

He wore his heavy overcoat and was turning his hat over in his hands. His cheeks were flushed and vibrant from the chill of the outdoors. "May I come in?"

"Of course," she replied without hesitating, and stepped aside.

He entered and set his hat down on a chair, removed his coat and wasted no time before beginning to explain the reason for his visit.

"I learned something today," he said. "Something my brothers do not know—at least not yet—and since we are legally betrothed I feel you have a right to know."

There was something rather alarming in his voice, as if it were an emergency of some sort. With a pang of concern, she gestured toward the chairs in front of the fire. He went to sit down and warmed his hands while Anne took a seat across from him. "Should I send for tea, or something stronger?"

He shook his head. Then he lounged back in the chair and ran a hand through his thick golden hair.

Heaven help her, it was not easy to focus on the matter at hand when he was sprawled in the chair looking like a beautiful lion and all she wanted to do was lunge forward and rip his waistcoat open, slide her hands up under his shirt, and press her lips to his chest.

Anne cleared her throat. "What happened?"

He let out a sigh. "Sometimes I wonder if there are certain things in life that one is better off not knowing."

"What do you mean?"

He reached for both her hands and held them. "I just spoke to my mother and learned the identity of my real father."

A log shifted on the grate and sparks flew up the chimney. Anne regarded him thoughtfully.

"That's good news, isn't it?" she said. "Or perhaps you're trying to tell me it's not. What happened between them? Who is it? Are you at liberty to tell me?"

"Believe it or not," he replied, "it is someone you have met. Someone who knows my father quite intimately." He paused, then shook his head again, as if he could not believe it himself.

"Is it Dr. Thomas?" she asked.

His eyes lifted. "Is it that obvious? Was I a fool not to see it sooner?"

"Of course not. He is the only person I have met who seems a likely candidate." She waited for Garrett to say something more, but he continued to rub the pads of his thumbs over her palms.

"Are they together now?" she asked. "Are they lovers?"

"She assures me they are just friends, but she also confessed that she does still love him and that he was the man she wanted to marry from a very young age."

"What else did she tell you about it?"

He inhaled deeply. "She explained that they were raised in the same county, and he was the son of a viscount. Her father seemed agreeable to the match until the illustrious Duke of Pembroke set eyes on her in a London ballroom and decided he had to have her as his duchess. He immediately made an offer and her father demanded that she accept. She felt duty-bound to obey, meanwhile Dr. Thomas was being strong-armed to join the army." Garrett bowed his head. "It seems the whole world was against them. Dr. Thomas later defied his father and went to medical school instead, was disowned and disinherited, so any hopes my mother clung to—that her own father might change his mind and allow her to marry the great love of her life—were lost.

They were separated for almost ten years, but she never quite got over him."

"Then what happened?"

"After providing three heirs to the Pembroke dukedom, she was abandoned by her husband in all ways. He resided in London, took an endless string of mistresses, and she was left to endure the humiliation of his indiscretions and excessive drinking. Eventually there came a night when she couldn't endure it any longer and she left him. Mother says she saddled a horse and rode hard to reach Dr. Thomas, who promised to help her escape the life that had been so cruelly forced upon her. She was going to ask the duke for a divorce, but it never came to that. After a week away from Pembroke, she missed her boys—my three older brothers—and knew the duke would never let her see them again if she divorced him. So she left Dr. Thomas and returned home. Nine months later she gave birth to Charlotte and me."

"My word," Anne said, leaning back in her chair. "Did the duke know the truth?"

Garrett nodded. "Yes, and he accepted us as his own only to avoid a scandal. As for Dr. Thomas, he was quite devastated when she returned to Pembroke, determined to be a faithful wife. Consequently he never married. Since he couldn't be with the woman he loved, he devoted his life to the study of medicine and the human brain. At one time, she needed his help when I was very ill as a child, and he managed my care. I vaguely remember certain details about his kindness. Then last spring—to help the very man who stole her away from him—he was steadfast in his duties to help the duke. Mother said he has been a godsend, and I confess, I must agree."

Anne closed her eyes, raised Garrett's hand to her lips and kissed it. "Oh, my darling. What will you do? Have you told Dr. Thomas that you know the truth?"

Silence. No response.

When she opened her eyes, Garrett was watching her mouth. Her heart began to race as he slowly, gently

stroked his thumb across her chin and along the line
of her jaw. His eyes glimmered with desire.

She wanted so badly to be practical about this man,
but every time he touched her, or simply looked at her
as he was looking at her now, she melted into a puddle
of intense yearning.

Garrett sat forward on the edge of his chair and
cupped her face in his hands. His lips touched hers in a
soft, brush-like stroke of teasing allure. The sizzling heat
of his lips caused a spark of electricity to explode in her
veins and shoot all the way down to her toes. She was
easily enticed out of her chair and before she realized
it, Garrett was easing her down onto the soft mattress
and covering her body with his own.

"Garrett," she whispered as she wrapped her legs
around him and tore his jacket off his shoulders. "How
do you do this to me? I cannot think straight when you
touch me."

With a husky groan of exertion, he tugged her skirts
up around her hips and wrestled with the fastenings of
his trousers.

Now, she didn't care about foreplay. All she wanted
was the swift, immediate sensation of his body entering
her own.

When their clothing was out of the way he rose up
on both arms and looked into her eyes while he shifted
his hips to position himself at the entrance to her
womanhood.

Already slick with desire, she welcomed him when he
thrust slowly forward with tantalizing ease.

"It feels good," she whispered in a mindless haze of
rapture.

He moved inside her smoothly, in and out, for a long
while as passion built ... until at last, the orgasm came.
She could not fathom the intensity of it, the searing
pleasure of the friction and heat—nor could she understand how he made her experience such feelings of love
when they barely knew each other ... when she had

accepted that he did not want her beyond these two brief weeks of engagement.

She lifted her hips to meet the fierce thrust of his passions and cried out in ecstasy as their lovemaking reached a fevered pitch.

God, how she'd wanted him.

Worse yet, she wanted to *tell* him how she felt, but she could not. She had to bite back the words that nearly spilled from her lips while she was pulsing in the throes of that incomprehensible rapture. *I love you*, she wanted to say. *I love you* ...

His orgasm followed hers almost instantly—as if he were pushed over the brink by the sounds of her panting moans and the violent tensing of her body all around him.

His seed spilled into her vigorously. She felt the hot gush of it reach her womb and was only half-conscious of the risk they had taken—because it felt so blissfully perfect.

She wasn't worried that a child might result.

She would have her own money.

She would raise it on her own ...

"God in heaven." Garrett groaned as he collapsed heavily upon her.

They were still dressed in their everyday clothes, and though it was the dead of winter, she felt hotter than the sun as she lay beneath him. His body heat was contagious.

As they lay in the afternoon light, weak and satiated, the fire crackled heartily in the grate.

Anne didn't know what to say. She was too busy wrestling with her guilt—for, though she knew she shouldn't have, she had given herself to this man, yet again, willingly and wantonly. Surely he must think her deserving of her scandalous reputation?

But what did he expect? Coming here to tell her the tragic tale of his mother and the great love of her life, and how they were torn apart by circumstances beyond their control ...

It was not unlike what Anne was feeling at the moment and what she would likely experience when they parted after their wedding day. Yet their situation was not beyond their control. If Garrett loved her, there was no reason why they could not be together. They could be man and wife and everyone, surely, would applaud their decision. What a dream come true that would be.

He rolled off her just then and let out an exhausted sigh. "Sometimes I wonder if you are some sort of angel sent from heaven to rescue me."

He turned his head on the pillow to look at her. She was surprised to find him frowning.

"Before I arrived here," he said, "all I wanted to do was leave again as soon as possible, but you have pulled me in."

"Are you sure it's me?" she replied. "I think you have been pulled in by your entire family. Even your father."

"Which one?" he asked with a bitter note of disdain that she understood was not directed at her, but rather, at the circumstances.

"The one who raised you," she replied. "And it's perfectly understandable for you to be angry. I am glad you came here to tell me about it. I think it's going to take a while for it to sink in. It's a lot to absorb in one day."

She rolled to face him and toyed flirtatiously with his neck cloth. "I am pleased I could at least provide you with some distraction just now, because it was quite enjoyable for me, as well."

His eyes smiled at her. "See what I mean? You are an angel, Anne. I feel like I could tell you anything and you would find the hope or humor in it. You don't judge me or anyone else. I've never met a woman quite like you."

She rested her cheek on the palm of her hand. "Not even your fiancée?"

He blinked a few times then gazed up at the ceiling again. "Oh, Anne. There are still things I haven't told you, and I wouldn't blame you if you decided to run as far away from me as you possibly can."

"What things?"

He laughed bitterly and did not answer the question.

"Please tell me," she pressed.

Garrett inhaled deeply, then spoke at last. "The woman I was pledged to marry was pregnant with my child. Otherwise ..." He paused.

"Yes?"

He shook his head. "It kills me to say these words when she is gone because of me, but that is the only reason we were going to marry. I don't think she loved me any more than I loved her, which was not very much. But she read my letters from Pembroke and discovered the fact that my brothers wanted me to marry by Christmas in order to save our fortune, and that there would be a large settlement bestowed upon me if I took a wife. Above all, my family connections and the lure of wealth meant more to her than I did."

"How did you become entangled with her?"

He closed his eyes and pinched the bridge of his nose. "It was a brief affair. She was newly divorced and leapt into bed with me for revenge on her husband. When I told her I had no intention to take a wife just to receive a settlement, she conveniently became pregnant. I couldn't leave her to raise the child alone. She wasn't as strong and independent as you. She was ... *emotional.*"

Anne laid her hand on Garrett's shoulder and wondered what giant confession he would make next. Good God, he really did need an angel to guide him through all this.

"Just as I thought," she gently said. "You are an honorable gentleman after all, fully prepared to sacrifice your freedom to rescue a damsel in distress."

"Is that what you think?" he asked. "Here is the worst part. There were moments when I wished something terrible would happen to release me from my obligation. Once, I imagined her falling from a horse and losing the child. How honorable is that?"

She swallowed uneasily. "You felt trapped."

He nodded, and suddenly she understood why he had been so mistrustful of her when he first arrived. He had been burned recently by a scheming woman who only wanted him for his inheritance.

Anne was not so very different. That's all she wanted, too.

"You mustn't blame yourself," she said. "The accident was not your fault, and you mustn't forget that you were prepared to do the honorable thing, despite your reservations."

He gazed up at the canopy. "You are certainly no damsel in distress, Anne. To the contrary, you are as sure and steady as a rock, and I am glad my brothers chose you."

A rock. If only he knew the truth—that she was trembling inside. Trembling with love and a dreadful, all-consuming fear that he would leave her after their wedding night, and she would never see him again. That fear had nothing to do with the money of course. She would give it all up if she could have his heart.

"I am glad too," she replied as she laid a kiss on his cheek. "I have not been this happy in a long time."

Not ever, if she were being completely honest, but something held her back from an overly excessive declaration of love. He'd said it all. He enjoyed her company because she did not place any romantic demands on him. She was solid as a rock. Emotionally self-sufficient and independent.

The dinner gong rang just then to signal it was time to dress.

"You had better go," she said, "before my maid walks through that door and swoons when she discovers I have a man in my bed."

He began to quickly fasten his trousers. "I thought we might have more time. I'm not ready to go yet."

Determined to spin a lighter mood on the moment, she sat up and said, "That is rather presumptuous, sir. Perhaps I am fully satisfied."

He sat up as well and stared at her intently. "Are you? Are you *truly* satisfied?"

Anne found she could not tell a lie. Not to Garrett. "No. I still want more."

He kissed her deeply, then drew back and cupped her cheek in his hand. "Can I come to you again tonight?"

She should tell him no. She should not be so available. She should make him work harder to win her affections. But in the end, none of that reached her lips, for she could not bear to waste a single moment with him. She wanted to make the most of these last few days and remember them forever.

"Yes, please come to me," she said. "I will wait up for you."

He kissed her briefly, then rose from the bed and quickly left her chamber. Two minutes later, her maid arrived to help her dress for dinner.

☙❦❧

Garrett walked into his bedchamber, shut the door and tugged at his neck cloth, which felt excessively tight.

Tossing it onto the bed, he breathed deeply and grabbed hold of the thick bedpost. He shut his eyes.

Her touch ... her lips ... her body ... her mind. His desire for her was unfathomable. He had not expected any of this when he returned home to secure his inheritance. He had not expected to feel such compassion for the father who had always treated him with disdain, like a street urchin. Nor had he expected to discover that his true father by blood was a brilliant physician and still devoted to his mother after a lifetime spent apart.

Most of all, he had not expected to fall in love with the woman his brothers had selected for him. He'd thought it would be a contractual agreement, nothing more. But he realized he had fallen completely, absolutely, head over heels in love, and felt like a foolish, heartsick schoolboy.

What would happen if he declared his affections and suggested they continue with the charade until their passion ran its course? She was resistant in so many ways. Would he frighten her off? It was difficult to say.

She cared for him. She was attracted to him. There was no doubt about that. Their lovemaking was like an exploding powder keg.

But what about the contract? Where would he draw the line? He hadn't agreed to this charade because he wanted a real marriage, but after listening to his mother talk about the lost love of her life, he found himself imagining a similar fate—his own future without Anne—and that was a difficult spoonful to swallow. He simply wasn't ready to walk away from her.

Perhaps there was hope for him yet. Perhaps this was a sign? There had to be a reason why she'd entered his life now, of all times—when he hadn't been able to escape the constant sickening sense that he was back with his boat, gasping for air, sinking to the bottom of the sea.

Had God truly sent him a Christmas angel to pull him up to the surface?

Perhaps there was some other purpose he was meant to serve.

Feeling eager and cautiously hopeful for the first time in his life, Garrett rang for his valet and quickly dressed for dinner.

Chapter Thirteen

*A*NNE QUIVERED WITH ecstasy a few nights later as Garrett rolled off her and lay on his back beside her, still clasping her hand tenderly.

On this particular night, he had come to her bed-chamber almost immediately after dinner, and they tore at each other's clothes until they were naked and writhing passionately on the bed—which all happened in a matter of minutes.

There had been nothing hurried about it once they lay together in each other's arms. The foreplay was impressive and wonderfully pleasurable, with teasing hands, roving tongues and hungry mouths. By the time Garrett climaxed inside her—again without any protection against a pregnancy—she experienced her third orgasm of the day and began to wonder if she had died and gone to heaven.

"How is this possible?" she asked, panting from the exertion of their lovemaking. "You make me forget what day it is. I'm not even sure I can remember my name. My brain has turned to mush."

He, too, was working to catch his breath. "I thought dinner would never end. All I could think about was how long it would take me to unbutton your gown."

She chuckled softly. "You must have been practicing in your head because you were faster than a bullet."

He turned his head on the pillow to look at her. "But the rest wasn't too fast, I hope. I've been selfish with you these past few days. I wanted to take my time tonight."

"You did." With a languorous smile, she rolled to face him. "And you've always taken time where it counts, Garrett. You seem to make it last just the right amount.

I feel very satisfied . . . yet I want more. After a brief rest, of course."

He gathered her into his arms and she snuggled closer. Running her fingers across the smooth planes of his chest and drawing tiny circles around his nipples with the tip of her finger, she marveled at his physical perfection. He was the most beautiful man she had ever known.

"Are you ready for tomorrow?" she asked, referring of course to their wedding ceremony which would take place in less than twenty-four hours.

"More than ready," he replied, wrapping both arms around her. "I have absolutely no reservations. What about you? Are *you* ready?"

"Of course. It's what we agreed to, and it has all been wonderful, Garrett."

She felt incredibly relaxed.

"Do you find it strange," he asked, rubbing his thumb lightly over her shoulder, "that we have been making love, when that was not part of the contract?"

Not entirely sure where this was going, Anne took great care with her reply. "Perhaps a little, but we are attracted to each other. I don't regret it, if that's what you're asking."

"No, that's not what I'm asking."

Anne cleared her throat. "Are you going to elaborate?"

Garrett rose up on an elbow and ran a hand down over her hip. "I love every soft curve of your body . . . the fragrance of your skin, and the silky feel of your hair when it brushes across my face."

He hadn't answered the question, but she didn't mind when he spoke words like that—words that made her melt into him and feel as if she could stay in bed with him forever.

His eyes met hers. "What would you say if I suggested that we become rebels and break the rules of the contract?"

Her heart began to pound. "In what way?"

All of a sudden, she was no longer relaxed. Her hopes were soaring, yet she was still fighting to grab hold of them, pull them to the ground, and stomp on them. She couldn't bear if he referred to something different from what she wanted.

True love. Commitment. A devotion that would last a lifetime.

"What if we didn't part ways after the wedding?" he added. "What if we stayed together for a while?"

Anne wet her lips and labored to appear calm about his proposition.

"I'm not ready for this to end," he continued. "I like being with you. You like being with me as well, do you not?"

"Of course," she replied.

"Then let us continue with the charade." He paused. "Forgive me, that is not what I meant. It is not a charade. It is very real. I am passionate about you Anne, and if I am to be honest, I will confess that I want more. I *need* more. I was feeling quite dead inside until I met you. Somehow you have awakened me to good things in my life. I feel reborn. So much has happened this past week, and you have been at the center of it all."

Every word he spoke was like music to her ears. She could hardly breathe ... But what did this mean? A few more weeks of lovemaking until he was recovered from all the turmoil in his life, and ready to leave? That would only prolong the agony of her dread—for surely one day it would end. If not tomorrow, then a few weeks from now, or perhaps even a year hence. The contract gave him the right to return to his bachelor life. Could she survive the loss of him one day in the future, when each day made her love him more than the last?

"Where is this headed?" she asked.

He shook his head. "I don't know exactly. I'm confused by this. It's not what I expected."

"Nor I." She pushed him aside so she could sit up and reach for her dressing gown, which was laid out on the chair beside the bed. She stood and slipped into it, tied the sash, and moved to the chair in front of the fire. There, she sat down and crossed one leg over the other.

She heard the sound of the bed covers rustling and the creak of the mattress as Garrett also rose to his feet.

He was naked. She was afraid to look at him, afraid to get sucked back in again. She must keep her wits about her, because he was everything she could ever dream of. What should she do? Surrender to loving him for as long as he wanted her?

Or protect herself?

When at last she looked at him, she was relieved to see that he had pulled the coverlet off the bed and wrapped himself in it. Thank God it was winter.

He knelt down before her. "What's wrong? Have I asked too much of you? I know you wish to be independent and I respect that, but you mean a great deal to me. I don't want to lose you. I want to be a part of your life."

He reached out to hold her hand.

"I don't want to lose you either," she carefully replied, without spilling all her emotions onto the floor. She must stay calm and maintain her dignity. "But being a part of my life isn't good enough, Garrett. I will be your wife in name only—I have agreed to that—but I cannot stay with you 'for a while,' as you put it. That would make me your temporary mistress. Do not misunderstand. I am not angry. This has been very enjoyable and I have no regrets, but when this engagement comes to an end, it must be all or nothing after that. If we are to be united in name only, then I must insist that we stay true to the terms of the agreement, for I cannot settle for less."

He rose up and took the seat across from her. "I see."

For a long time they sat before the fire, saying nothing.

Anne was not surprised by his lack of response, for he had been clear about his goals from the beginning. Now he wanted to be with her until the passion ran its course, then cite the terms of the contract, reclaim his freedom, and that would be the end of it.

Though considered damaged goods by some, in her heart, she truly believed she was worth more than that.

Their eyes met and he stared at her for a long time while his expression remained impassive. Unreadable.

Anne's heart beat frantically. Perhaps all he needed was more time. Had she spoiled everything by giving him an ultimatum?

"It's past midnight," he said in a suddenly casual tone. "Isn't there a rule about not seeing your intended on the day you walk down the aisle? Isn't it supposed to be bad luck?"

She fought to breathe normally and rose from her chair. "Yes, that's what they say."

"Then I should return to my own room." Turning, he went to fetch his clothes, then added lightly, "I wouldn't want to take any chances, tempt fate . . . evoke the curse or something."

Anne watched him get dressed and could have wept as an awkward silence poured into the room. Everything had been so perfect, but then she had demanded all or nothing.

She kissed him good-bye at the door and worried that she had asked too much of him, and had already received her answer—and it was not the answer she had been hoping for.

Chapter Fourteen

GARRETT WOKE AT dawn the following morning to the astounding reality that it was his wedding day. It hardly seemed possible, and he felt both astonished and transformed—for he was passionately in love with his bride. When he rose from bed and walked to the window, it was as if he were seeing the sunrise for the first time.

There was still something missing, however. Something he needed to add to the magic of this day ... Something he had to do.

A short while later, after he dressed and took a quick breakfast, he stepped onto the early morning train with a strange mixture of bewilderment and awe. So much had happened over the past two weeks. He had come home to a father who had changed considerably since the last time they'd spoken. The duke was no longer a tyrant, but instead was a frail, frightened man who remembered nothing of their former estrangement, and wanted Garrett, his youngest son, at his side.

Or perhaps the duke did remember their estrangement, and that was why he was so frightened of death, and of being alone. Hell was not a pleasant thing to dream about. Garrett understood that. He also understood the desire to atone.

The duke was coming to the end of his life. His mind was failing him. Garrett found he could no longer bear a grudge toward the man for his mistakes in the past. He felt compassion for him now.

More importantly, there was forgiveness. And if he could forgive his father, perhaps he could forgive himself, too.

As the train pulled away from the station, Garrett felt a renewed sense of purpose. This morning he would

travel to London to see Dr. Thomas. He would invite him
to attend the wedding.

The wedding . . .

That, above all, was at the heart of this awakening.
To be more specific, it was Anne. Anne, who harbored
no bitterness toward those who had wronged her. Anne,
who wanted a love that would last a lifetime. She did not
let her past define her.

It must be all or nothing.

He would not insult her honor by offering her less.
Today — if she would have him — he would become her
true husband in all ways and pledge his heart, body,
and soul to her until the end of time. He couldn't wait
to get down on one knee and propose to her properly,
in front of everyone. Pray God she would accept him.

ᗢᥴ᥎ᗷ

The train arrived at Paddington Station at 10:15 am.
Garrett shouldered his way through the crowd and
whistled for a hackney cab to take him to Dr. Thomas's
offices on Park Lane. Since he was arriving without an
appointment, and wasn't even certain if the clinic would
be open on Christmas Eve, he instructed the driver to
wait, for he might need to be taken to the doctor's private
residence in Mayfair.

He alighted from the vehicle and stepped onto the
frozen walk, felt the sharp winter chill on his cheeks,
and ventured inside.

As he closed the door behind him, he noticed a dis-
tinctive smell. Some sort of antiseptic perhaps, which
was both unfamiliar and strangely interesting. There
were a few ladies seated in chairs in a small waiting
area. He removed his hat and gloves, then approached
the desk to speak to a clerk, a young man with mustache
and spectacles.

"Is Dr. Thomas in this morning?"

The clerk glanced up. "Yes, sir, but only until noon as it's Christmas Eve, and I am afraid he is fully booked. Would you like to make an appointment for another day?"

Garrett tapped his gloves against his thigh. "It is a personal matter, and rather urgent. I would be grateful if you could inform him that I am here."

"Your name?"

"Lord Garrett Sinclair of Pembroke."

The color drained from the young man's face. He set down his pen. "Pembroke Palace?"

"Yes."

The clerk leapt to his feet. The chair legs scraped across the floor. "I do beg your pardon, my lord. Please forgive me. I will let him know you are here."

Garrett thanked the young man and turned to take a seat under a tall potted tree fern.

While he waited, he let his gaze peruse the waiting area. Across from him a woman held a young child on her lap. The child appeared sleepy. Feverish perhaps.

Another older woman was reading a book. He wondered what ailed her, for she looked perfectly healthy in every way.

He then noticed a painting on the wall and stood up to examine it more closely. It appeared to be an artistic rendering of the human anatomy. He found it quite fascinating and was still studying the details when a door opened in the back hall.

The clerk returned to the waiting room. "Dr. Thomas will see you now, my lord. If you will come this way."

Garrett followed the young man down a narrow, red-carpeted corridor. He peered into two empty examination rooms as they passed by. At the end of the hall, the clerk opened a heavy oak door and gestured for Garrett to wait inside. "This is the doctor's private office. He will be with you shortly."

"Thank you." Garrett entered the room and looked around at the dark green painted walls with tiger oak wainscoting, the piles of medical books in danger of toppling over on the sofa, and a set of tall bookcases on the far wall behind the large mahogany desk. Most notably, there was a life size skeleton on a stand by the window.

He strode to it immediately, reached out to touch the ribs, and discovered it was made of some sort of plaster.

Wildly curious, he couldn't resist the urge to examine the joints. He squatted down and studied the knees, then the ankles and spine. What a fascinating reproduction of the human body. He was completely mesmerized.

Next, his gaze lifted to a framed painting on the wall. This one depicted a team of surgeons crowded around a body in a lecture hall, performing some sort of procedure while students looked on. He leaned close and squinted, trying to make out what the doctors were doing with their instruments when the door opened. Garrett turned around.

Dr. Thomas paused at the threshold and regarded him with a look of pleasure. "Lord Garrett. How nice to see you."

Garrett stepped forward and held out his hand. "Nice to see you again, too, sir. I apologize for the interruption. I see you have patients waiting."

"Only two more this morning. My nurse is with them now. What can I do for you?" He strode to the desk and set down the file he was carrying. "Please take a seat."

Garrett sat in the leather chair in front of the desk while Dr. Thomas sat behind it.

Not quite sure how to begin, Garrett pointed at the skeleton. "That's quite interesting," he said. "You must find your profession very rewarding."

"I do indeed," Dr. Thomas replied. "What interests me most is that there never seems to be an end to the discoveries. I believe medical science is in its infancy. There are new diseases discovered and new theories formed every day. I am still a student in many ways. I suspect I always will be."

"That is remarkable. I am very impressed."

"And how is your father?" the doctor asked. "Is he recovering?"

"He's doing well," Garrett replied, "but I am here for a different reason, Dr. Thomas. It concerns something of a more ..." He paused. "A more personal nature."

Dr. Thomas leaned back in his chair and regarded Garrett uncertainly in the morning light streaming in through the paned window.

"I spoke to my mother yesterday," Garrett continued. "It was an important discussion, one I wish we'd begun many years ago, but unfortunately that was not to be. Nevertheless, I now know the truth about my parentage and since I am to be married today, it was important that I see you. Surely you can guess why?"

Dr. Thomas cleared his throat and kept his eyes fixed on Garrett's. "I believe I can. How much did your mother tell you?"

"Everything."

Giant snowflakes began to fall outside the window. Garrett watched them for a moment.

Again, nothing felt quite the same as it had a few short days ago.

Dr. Thomas relaxed in his chair. "I wasn't sure if she would ever tell you the whole truth. Mostly because I thought you might leave again after today, but I am pleased you know the particulars at last. It wasn't easy for either of us all those years ago."

"No, I should think not."

Garrett swallowed over a sudden wave of emotion that rose up within him. All his life he had known he was a bastard. His mother had showered him with love, of course, but not his father—never his father.

He didn't feel like a bastard now. He liked Dr. Thomas. He liked him very much. There was something about the doctor that made Garrett feel at ease ... made him want to embrace the future.

In that moment, sitting in his real father's office, he felt certain this was all meant to unfold exactly as it was unfolding. He wasn't sure why yet, but believed it would eventually become clear.

"I am not sure how to proceed," Dr. Thomas said. "It's Christmas Eve, and I feel very blessed. I am proud that you are my son, and that you know the truth at last. I hope we can come to know each other better."

"I would like that," Garrett replied, "which is why I have come. I wish to extend an invitation to you, sir. Would you attend my wedding to Lady Anne this evening? It would mean a great deal to me."

The doctor's eyes filled with warmth and happiness. "I would be honored, Garrett. What time?"

"Five pm," he replied, "but because Christmas is tomorrow, there is only one more train—at noon. It leaves from Paddington Station, and since I am the groom, I must be on it. Can you finish here in time and accompany me?"

Dr. Thomas stood up. "Absolutely. If you could wait here, I will be ready in half an hour."

"Excellent." Garrett stood up as well. "May I take a look at some of your medical books while I wait?"

"By all means," Dr. Thomas replied as he departed the room. "I will be back soon."

ᕕᘉᕗ

They caught the train in plenty of time and spent the two-hour journey talking about Dr. Thomas's life as a young man and his decision to enter the field of medicine. Then they discussed Garrett's childhood and his recent years in Greece.

Garrett told him about the boating accident. Dr. Thomas was sympathetic and urged Garrett to remember that he had done everything he could to save the boat and the passengers on board.

"Sometimes, nature is a beast," he said, "and tragedy is unavoidable. I see a great deal of it in my profession, and I have learned that most of us must face some form of challenge in our lives. But without hardship, we wouldn't learn and grow."

Garrett absorbed every word of his father's advice and reflected carefully about the accident for the remainder of the trip back to Pembroke. He thought about the settlement he would receive for marrying Anne today, and was more determined than ever to share it with Georgina's family. Nothing could ever replace what they had lost, but it would at least ease Garrett's conscience to know they would have no financial worries in the future.

By the time the train pulled into the village station, the snow was falling fast and the temperature had dropped. Garrett had previously arranged for the palace coach to be waiting. He and the doctor hurried through the biting wind and snow to reach it at the curb.

The driver was hunched over with his coat collar pulled tight around his chin, his wool scarf wrapped around his face to shield against the storm.

"It's a fine day for a wedding, my lord!" he said good-naturedly as he tipped his hat at Garrett.

"Quite right, Jameson! How were the roads?"

"They were passable getting here, but we should leave without delay. Wouldn't want you to be late for your own wedding!"

"Certainly not." Garrett swung inside, where it was warm and sheltered from the wind.

He took a seat across from Dr. Thomas, who removed his hat and brushed the snowflakes off the brim.

"Are you nervous?" he asked with a teasing smile.

Garrett shook his head. "Not in the least. I cannot imagine marrying a more perfect woman. Odd, really. I'd always imagined one's wedding day to be a daunting affair, but it's not daunting at all. It feels right in every way."

Dr. Thomas regarded him with understanding. "I know that feeling, as I felt it once myself, many years ago."

The coach lurched forward and they drove past the snow-covered village green, then traveled down the hill beyond the mercantile and entered the woods.

Chapter Fifteen

"*STOP! PLEASE STOP!*"

At the sound of a voice on the road, Garrett slid across the seat and used his sleeve to rub at the fog on the window.

He peered out at a young boy in a short black coat, his red scarf flying in the wind. He had come out of the woods and was running alongside the coach.

Garrett stood up and pounded on the roof. "Hold up, Jameson!"

The coach pulled to a halt. Garrett flung the door open and jumped into the snow. Its depth caught him by surprise, for it nearly reached his knees.

The boy grabbed hold of his sleeve. "Please help me, sir! My brother fell through the ice! I tried to help him but I can't get him out!"

Garrett immediately sought more information. "Where is he? At the fish pond?"

"Yes, sir!" The boy turned and pointed into the forest. "Just through there! I told him it wasn't safe, but he wouldn't listen!"

Garrett turned to Dr. Thomas as he stepped out of the vehicle. "Did you hear that?"

"Yes. We must hurry."

"Jameson!" Garrett shouted. "A boy has fallen through the ice at the fish pond! Hand me your horsewhip and secure the team. Then follow us. We will most likely need your help."

The coachman tossed the whip to Garrett and climbed down from the box.

Garrett and Dr. Thomas trudged through the snow into the shelter of the trees to follow the boy.

It seemed a terrible distance through stinging sleet to reach the pond. When at last they emerged through a heavy curtain of pine boughs, the wind was gusting like a fiend across the wide circle of ice.

"Good God," Garrett said as he spotted the boy half submerged. He was not fighting to climb out. Was he even conscious?

"You there!" Dr. Thomas shouted, rushing forward. "Can you hear me?" The boy's head lifted slightly. Dr. Thomas swung around. "He won't last much longer."

Garrett handed the coiled horsewhip to him. "I will crawl out to reach the boy. Throw me this line if I have trouble."

Stepping onto the ice, Garrett bounced lightly to test his weight. It seemed secure.

"I'm coming!" he shouted to the boy as he leapt lightly across the frozen, snow-covered surface.

He dropped to his stomach as he drew near and crawled as close as he dared. "Grab my hand! Hurry!"

The boy was shivering violently. He lifted his eyes.

"I'm here to help you," Garrett said. "Take hold of my hand and I will pull you out."

"I…I c…can't," the boy stammered through chattering teeth as he shook his head.

"Yes, you can. Your brother's waiting for you. He's watching from the bank." Garrett slid closer on his stomach and grabbed hold of the boy's wrist. "I've got you now, but I can't pull you out on my own. You need to kick. Can you do that?"

The boy weakly kicked with his legs. It wasn't enough. Garrett reached out, hand over hand, to take hold of his arm and pulled with all his might, but he had no traction, no leverage. The boy's eyes fell closed and he began to sink back, pulling Garrett with him.

Suddenly he was back on the deck of his boat. Johnny was laughing in the sun and the wind. It was such a perfect day. There was not a cloud in the sky …

Then the wretched look of terror in Johnny's eyes as the wreckage pulled him into the dark stormy depths. *I've got you ... I won't let go ... hold on tight ...*

Grounding himself in the present, Garrett turned and shouted through the raging sleet and snow. "We need help!"

By then Jameson had arrived. "On my way!" He skidded fearlessly onto the ice, dove onto his belly and slid close enough to grab hold of Garrett's leg.

Next, Dr. Thomas carefully trotted out and took hold of Jameson's boot. Together they formed a human chain and pulled hard, grunting against the strain until the boy was drawn out of the hole. He opened his eyes and woke up.

"Can you walk?" Garrett asked.

"I...I don't know." His eyes rolled back in his head again.

The ice creaked and shifted beneath them. There was no more time. Garrett stood up, grabbed hold of the boy's arm and hauled him quickly up onto the snowy bank and to the treeline.

They rolled him onto his back. "He's not conscious," Garrett said, tapping the boy's cheek. "Wake up! Can you hear me? Wake up!"

"What's wrong with him?" the younger brother cried. "Is he going to be all right?"

Dr. Thomas leaned in, pressed his fingers to the pulse at the boy's neck and lowered his ear to listen. "He's still breathing, but his pulse is weak. We need to get him out of these wet clothes. Help me carry him back to the coach."

Garrett scooped the boy into his arms, wrapped him against his chest under his greatcoat, then began the difficult trek through the woods and back to the main road. The wind was against them and every step forward was like walking through water. Visibility was poor and it seemed to take forever to reach the road.

Jameson opened the door of the coach and helped Garrett lift the boy inside. He was so very heavy because of all the water in his clothes.

Garrett set him down on the seat. Dr. Thomas entered behind them, removed the boy's sodden coat and shirt, then shrugged out of his own coat and wrapped it around the boy.

"Where do you live?" he asked the younger brother while he retrieved his black leather medical bag from under the seat. As he withdrew his stethoscope he asked, "How old are you and what are your names?"

"I'm Joshua Callaghan and I'm eleven," he replied. "My brother is Marcus. He's thirteen and we live at the end of Jacoby Lane, near the river."

Dr. Thomas glanced at Garrett. "How far is that?"

"Not far. About two miles."

"Is that the nearest cottage?" he asked.

Garrett turned questioningly to Jameson who was now standing in the snow outside the door.

"It's closer than the village," Jameson told them, "but I don't trust that old cart road. The storm is getting worse. It might be best to stay on this road and return to the village. We could go straight to the local doctor."

"Does he have a well-stocked medical office?" Dr. Thomas asked.

"I believe so, and he should be there, as he lives on the upper floor."

"That sounds like the best option, then," Dr. Thomas replied. "Take us there, Jameson, as quickly as possible, if you please." Then he glanced across at Garrett with some concern. "I fear you may be late for your wedding."

Garrett laid a comforting hand on Joshua's shoulder. "Anne will understand."

"But your inheritance ... Perhaps you could take one of the horses and go on yourself."

"No," Garrett firmly replied. "Jameson will need both horses to bring this coach to the village. I won't leave you, sir. Or them." He glanced down at the two young brothers.

The coach rumbled forward into a clearing where Jameson turned them around to head back in the other direction.

ᘓᘏᘍᘓ

They were halfway to the village when Dr. Thomas checked Marcus's pulse again.

He leaned down to listen at the boy's mouth and nose, then tore the extra coat off him to listen to his chest.

"What's wrong?" Garrett asked.

"He's not breathing." Dr. Thomas placed the stethoscope over his heart. "I'm not hearing a heartbeat."

Joshua began to weep. Garrett gathered the younger boy into his arms. "There must be something we can do. When I was in your office this morning, I read something about resuscitating drowning victims. If we blow into his mouth, won't he start breathing again?"

"He didn't drown," Dr. Thomas replied, shaking Marcus violently. "There is no water in his lungs. It's the cold. It has slowed his body functions. Now his heart is not circulating his blood. Getting him warm again is our best hope."

Garrett frowned. "Surely there must be some way to revive him?"

Dr. Thomas shook Marcus again. "His heart needs to beat. Wake up, Marcus! Wake up!" He laid the boy down, leaned over him, pressed a fist to his chest and began to push in a steady rhythm.

"What are you doing?" Garrett asked.

"I'm trying to help his heart. Come on Marcus!"

Garrett watched, transfixed as Dr. Thomas continued to push on the boy's chest repeatedly with the heel of his hand. Then he grabbed hold of Marcus's shoulders, sat him up again, and roughly shook him.

"Have you ever done this before?" Garrett asked.

"No."

"You're hurting him!" Joshua cried.

Dr. Thomas laid Marcus down again, applied the stethoscope, and listened. For a long moment he was quiet, then he blinked a few times. "There! I heard a beat! A single heartbeat!"

They all stared in silence with breath held, waiting . . .

He said nothing for a few more seconds.

"Another!"

Dr. Thomas turned to Joshua. "Come here, boy. Take off your jacket. Lie beside him and hug him as tight as you can."

"But he's dead!" Joshua sobbed.

"No, his heart wants to work. We just need to get him warm. Come on now, that's a good boy. Hold him tight. Don't let go."

Garrett moved to the window and wiped his sleeve frantically on the foggy pane. "We're almost there. Just another few minutes . . ."

Dr. Thomas continued to monitor Marcus's pulse until they pulled to a halt in front of the local doctor's office and residence.

Garrett opened the door and leapt out. The wind and snow nearly knocked him over. The blizzard had worsened, and he was forced to accept the fact that he would not likely make it back to the palace by midnight.

He prayed Anne would understand, and that his father would not see it as a sign of the curse. God knows what he might do.

Thrusting those thoughts aside for the moment, he trudged through the deep snow and pounded on the door. "Is anyone here? We have a sick child!"

When no one answered, he tried the door but it was locked. He moved to the window, cupped his hands to the frosty glass, and peered inside. The office was dark and deserted. He backed up and looked at the second story window. All the curtains were drawn. "Dammit!"

Desperately he turned around to see Jameson lifting Marcus out of the coach.

Garrett glanced to the left and saw a wrought iron chair half buried in the snow. He hurried to it, tried to pull it free, but it was embedded in the ice. He kicked it fiercely until he knocked it over, then hoisted it over his head, hauled it to the window and swung hard to smash the glass.

Garrett cleared the broken shards away with his sleeve, crawled through and hurried through the parlor to open the front door.

Jameson was there waiting. "Well done, my lord." He carried the unconscious boy inside. "Where should I lay him down?"

"Over there." Garrett pointed to the examination table.

Dr. Thomas and Joshua hurried in behind them. Dr. Thomas took a quick look at what supplies were available, but seemed most relieved to find the grate already piled high with fresh kindling.

"This will do," he said as he removed his coat. "Someone get a fire going. We need heat and hot water." He studied the younger boy who stood at his brother's side, a worried look on his face and tears in his eyes. "Child, find a place by the hearth and warm yourself while we see to your brother."

"I'll take care of the fire," Garrett said. "Jameson, go and cover that broken window."

They all quickly set about their tasks.

Chapter Sixteen

*F*OR A FEW brief moments that afternoon, Anne had looked outside at the snowy landscape and was tempted toward cowardice. She had thought about ordering a carriage and leaving before the ceremony could take place. But how could she give up the money? And where in the world would she go without it?

It was fear that made her want to run, plain and simple, for she never imagined she would fall so deeply and passionately in love.

It had seemed such a simple affair when Lord Hawthorne and Lord Blake presented their proposal: take part in a mock engagement, sign a marriage certificate, have relations with a man she'd never see again, accept a large sum of money, then begin a new life.

Now she sat before the looking glass wearing Charlotte's stunning white wedding gown and wanted only to find Garrett waiting for her at the altar—with love and desire in his eyes.

The wind gusted outside the window and the sharp sleet pelted the glass. It had turned into quite a blizzard. She was thankful there were no guests scheduled to arrive. It would be a small private ceremony for members of the immediate family only.

A knock sounded at her door. "Come in!"

Charlotte entered wearing a lovely pale blue gown with silver trimmings. Her hair was swept into a loose twist on top of her head with tiny white flowers woven through the locks.

"Hello Anne," she said as she moved to the chair before the roaring fire and sat down.

"If you've come to ensure that I am not late for my own wedding," Anne said, "you will be pleased to see that I am quite ready."

Charlotte cleared her throat. "That's wonderful, but ..." She paused. "There is a slight problem. None of us wanted to mention anything before now because we didn't wish to alarm you, but judging by the hour, I think it's high time someone told you the truth."

Anne's belly performed a rather sickening flip. "What truth?"

"It's Garrett. I don't know how to say this, but ... he's not here."

Anne frowned. "What do you mean? The wedding is in one hour. Where is he?"

Charlotte took a breath. "We're not sure, exactly. All we know is that he had a driver take him to the train station early this morning. He was headed for London."

"London!"

"Yes, but do not despair. We spoke to Jameson before noon, and he informed us that Garrett instructed him to pick him up upon his return."

"Did Jameson follow his instructions?"

"That is the problem, you see. Jameson has not returned either. This afternoon's two o'clock train was the last arrival of the day."

Had he turned his back on her? A flash memory of that day in church pounded through Anne's brain. *Harlot, you are not welcome here.*

Was this another punishment for her sins in the past? For her terrible naivety?

No, she would not believe it.

Anne strove to remain calm. "Something must have happened. The weather is very bad. They must be delayed because of the snow."

"That is quite possible," Charlotte agreed, "which is why we have sent out a few grooms on horseback to search before it gets dark. There is only the one main road from here to the village station, so if they are stuck in the snow, we will find them."

But what if they aren't? Anne wondered frantically. What if Garrett never returned from London? What if he changed his mind about going through with this sham of a wedding, as she had considered doing earlier that afternoon? Was he headed for Greece?

Anne stood and walked to the window. She could barely see the first trees edging the drive, for the whole world had turned white.

No ... she would not accept that Garrett would leave her at the altar. He knew what she'd suffered before. He would never humiliate her that way. If he'd changed his mind, he would simply tell her. *Wouldn't he?*

She turned and faced Charlotte. "Something must have happened. I know Garrett. He wouldn't just leave us all in the lurch."

The clock was ticking, however. They had to marry by midnight or the terms of the duke's will would take effect immediately. If all four brothers were not married before Christmas Day, the entire unentailed fortune would be awarded to the London Horticultural Society, and the family would be almost broke.

"I hope you're right," Charlotte said with some uncertainty, "because I admit ... I am not so sure."

抗抗抗

At the sound of a whimper, Garrett rushed to Marcus's side and grabbed hold of his hand. The boy was as white as death, but at least he was breathing.

"My chest hurts," he complained. "Where am I?"

Overcome with relief, exhausted from the terrible ordeal of the past few hours—not knowing if the boy would live or die—Garrett bowed his head and said a quiet prayer of thanks.

He glanced up at the clock on the wall. It was just past midnight.

"You're at the doctor's office in Pembroke Village," he replied. "Do you remember what happened to you?"

"I fell through the ice."

Poor little Joshua was curled up asleep in the chair by the fire and did not wake. Dr. Thomas, however, who had gone to rest in the front parlor, came hurrying to the bedside.

"He's awake?"

"Yes. It's a Christmas miracle, to be sure," Garrett replied as he watched the doctor—his own brilliant father—examine the boy. "You saved his life."

Dr. Thomas's eyes lifted. "We both saved him." He leaned over Marcus's face and spoke distinctly. "How are you feeling, son? Can you tell me your name?"

"It's Marcus."

"Good. Do you know what day it is?"

"It's Christmas Eve. My pa is going to grind me up for dinner. Where's my brother?"

Dr. Thomas stroked the boy's hair away from his face. "By the hearth, and on the contrary, I think your father will be very happy to see you in the morning."

"Does he know I'm here?" Marcus asked.

"Not yet. The storm hasn't let up. We couldn't get you home, but we'll send Jameson out at first light."

At the sound of their voices, Joshua woke and wandered sleepily to the bedside. "Is he going to be all right?"

"He's going to be just fine," Dr. Thomas replied.

Garrett backed out of the way so Joshua could see his brother.

Thank you, God. Thank you for letting him live.

Later, after they transferred Marcus and his brother to a more comfortable bed in the next room, Garrett and Dr. Thomas sat before the fire sipping hot tea.

"What will happen with you?" Dr. Thomas asked. "You've missed your wedding and your father's deadline. Is there no way to plead for an extension? It was a matter of life and death. Surely the courts will consider that."

"Possibly," Garrett replied, "but at the present time I am more concerned with how Anne must be feeling, wondering why I wasn't there to marry her. I hope she will forgive me. And father must be beside himself; he was so frightened of the curse."

"If he is frightened, he will wake in the morning to discover the palace is still standing, strong and sure as ever."

They were quiet for a moment. "When will the fortune be transferred to the Horticultural Society?" Dr. Thomas asked.

"I'm not certain. My brothers will surely do their best to fight it in court, which could hold everything up." Garrett sipped his tea. "If only the money was going to a better cause—to feed the poor or build a new orphanage. Anything . . . But the *Horticultural Society*? As if England needs more flowers for the rich to enjoy."

Dr. Thomas considered that. "Perhaps you could convince them to put it to better use. Your mother has a few worthwhile charities that are near and dear to her heart. I'm sure the Society would consider contributing to some of those, out of respect for your family."

Garrett nodded. "That is an excellent idea." He stood up to check on Marcus in the next room. He was sleeping soundly, and his brother Joshua was curled up beside him.

"May I ask you something?" Garrett whispered to Dr. Thomas as he returned to his chair. "Did you know what you were doing when you pushed on Marcus's heart? Had you seen that done before?"

"No, and I had no idea if it would work, but I've been studying the human body all my life. It was instinct mostly—and desperation."

"You didn't give up. That's the important thing." Garrett leaned back in his chair again.

They sat in silence for another moment.

"Now may I ask *you* a question, Garrett?" the doctor asked.

"Of course."

"When your boat went down, did you work as hard to save those passengers as you worked to save Marcus today?"

Garrett experienced a flash memory of the giant waves, the ropes and canvas tangled together in the stormy sea, and how he had been pulled down into the cold dark depths.

Why had he been pulled down? Because he refused to let go of Johnny's hand. He'd sucked a few mouthfuls of water into his lungs and began to convulse before he finally let go and kicked his way to the surface.

"I risked my life," he replied. "But in the end I only saved myself."

"And you feel guilty about that?" Dr. Thomas said.

Garrett nodded.

"I understand, but it wasn't up to you to save everyone under those circumstances, son. I don't mean to sound disrespectful, but it's rather arrogant of you to think so. As I have said before, nature is both a beauty and a beast. You did your best, but it was simply their time that day, and not yours."

Garrett looked down at his tea that was now cold in the cup. "I suppose you've seen a lot of death in your profession ..."

"I have, and it is never easy, but it is a part of life. Sometimes, even when we do everything humanly possible to try and save someone, in the end, it makes no difference what we've done."

"It made a difference today."

"Yes, it did." Dr. Thomas closed his eyes, inhaled deeply, and slowly let it out.

Garrett watched him with interest. "I once told you that I envied your ability to cure people. I wonder if you might teach me some things?"

Dr. Thomas opened his eyes. "I'd be happy to." Then he smiled. "Or you could simply enrol in medical school. I could put in a good word for you."

Garrett stood up and walked to the window to look out at the storm. "It might not be such a bad idea to learn a profession," he said, "now that my family is broke."

Dr. Thomas sighed. "Money isn't everything, Garrett."

"I wholeheartedly agree," he replied, turning to face him. "It's one of the reasons why I left Pembroke Palace in the first place seven years ago. Despite the opulence and the endless flow of money, I wasn't happy."

Dr. Thomas squinted at him in the firelight. "A strange thing to hear from a man who agreed to marry a woman he never set eyes on before—for no other reason but to collect a monetary award the day after the wedding."

Garrett regarded him shrewdly. "Touché."

He returned to his chair and sat down.

"What are you going to do," Dr. Thomas asked, "now that there will be no funds awarded to you today?"

"I think the more important question," Garrett replied, "is what will Anne do?"

"It all depends on how you approach the situation."

"What do you recommend?"

The doctor considered the question for a moment, then offered his best fatherly advice. "I recommend extreme, heroic, and above all, desperate measures that may or may not involve groveling. To your betrothed, as well as your family members."

Garrett looked into the hot fire and suspected there could be no other cure for this. He thought of Anne, his beautiful Anne, and knew he would do anything to win her forgiveness.

What would it take? he wondered. How angry would she be?

Chapter Seventeen

THE STORM RAGED on through most of the night, but Christmas morning dawned with the blessings of a clear blue sky and a bright yellow sun casting its warmth upon the snow-covered grounds at Pembroke Palace.

Anne had waited up all night in the drawing room with Charlotte and the duchess, but fell asleep on the chaise longue when she could no longer keep her eyes from falling closed. She woke to find herself curled up on her side, still wearing her wedding gown and pearls. At some point, a kind soul had covered her with a woolen shawl.

She sat up quickly as it occurred to her that they had missed the deadline to save the Pembroke Palace fortune.

And Garrett had still not come home.

Dear Lord ...

She prayed that he had found shelter from the storm and that was the cause of the delay, rather than some other dreadful reason she did not dare confront.

But what if he did not return at all today? What would she do? How long would she wait?

Hearing the sound of a shovel scraping across the stone steps outside, she stood up and looked around the drawing room only to discover she was completely alone. The fire had died down hours ago. Charlotte and the duchess must have gone off to bed after she'd fallen asleep.

She walked slowly to the window and squinted in the bright sunlight that reflected off the snow. She glanced down at two servants shoveling snow off the steps below.

The forest in the distance was cloaked in white. It was the most beautiful Christmas morning she had ever beheld, yet her heart ached with painful thoughts of what might have kept Garrett from her. Was he all right? What if something terrible had happened?

She would give anything to know that he was unharmed. *Anything.* She would surrender her own happiness, return to her uncle's house in Yorkshire if she must, if only she could see Garrett walk through this door one more time. *Safe.*

Then suddenly a horse-drawn sleigh appeared in the distance, making its way slowly up the lane. Anne's heart leapt to her throat, and she pressed both hands to the glass.

Garrett. Please let it be you.

She didn't care if the contract was broken, or if there was no money, or even if their engagement charade was at an end forever. All that mattered was that he was alive and well.

She would find her own way to survive.

For a few more heart-pounding moments she watched the sleigh draw closer to the house. She was breathing quite heavily when it reached the steps.

There were two men in the sleigh, but they wore fur hats and the frost on the lower part of the glass window obscured her view.

Clutching the shawl about her shoulders, she dashed from the room and ran to the main staircase, flew down the red carpeted stairs like some sort of winged creature dressed in white, and hurried across the marble floor of the Great Hall.

Suddenly she realized the rest of the family had appeared and followed her down the stairs as well—the duchess, then Devon, Blake, and Charlotte.

The butler had already opened the double front doors. Anne darted out into the cold. She stopped under the wide portico as the two men stepped out of the sleigh, then breathed a sigh of relief when she recognized that incredibly handsome face.

Garrett looked up at her and laid a hand over his heart.

Her own heart melted, and she was so happy to see him! But what did it mean?

༭ళ౿

Anne truly was an angel sent from heaven, Garrett thought as he watched her dash down the stairs in a flowing white wedding gown and sky-blue shawl. The sight of her, after all he'd been through, was like a hot sunburst that exploded in his chest.

He did not wait for her to reach him at the sleigh. He took the steps two at a time to meet her half way. To his utter delight, she threw herself into his arms and hugged him so tight around the neck, he could barely breathe.

"Thank God you're safe," she said.

He drew back to look her in the eye, shocked and bewildered by her forgiveness, and then found himself admiring the gorgeous, tantalizing length of her body in that white dress.

"My God, you look beautiful." He forced his gaze back up to her face. "But you're not angry with me? I thought you might be, but there was no way to send word."

"Angry!" she replied, then seemed to realize what he was referring to. "Oh, yes. Yes, I am very angry about that. What woman wouldn't be?" She sighed. "Oh, Garrett. None of that matters. You're here now." She hugged him again. "Oh my word ... I am so sorry."

"*You're* sorry? Sorry for what?"

"We missed the deadline," she replied. "Your family's fortune ... The money you wanted ..."

He pulled her into his arms again. "I don't care about that, Anne. All that matters is that you are here, and you are not angry with me."

He held her tight, buried his face into her neck, breathed in the sweet scent of her skin. He couldn't seem to let go.

"Why did you believe I would be angry?" she softly asked.

He fought to gain control of his emotions. "Because it was money you wanted, too. For your freedom, Anne."

The others came rushing down the stairs just then, and his angel stepped out of his arms.

He knew instantly that it had been the wrong thing to say.

"Thank heavens you're all right!" Charlotte cried as she, too, launched herself into Garrett's arms.

"We were so worried," his mother said.

"What happened to you?" Devon asked.

Devon held out his hand to Dr. Thomas who had stayed back to give Garrett a moment alone with Anne. He was only just then reaching them on the steps. "Merry Christmas, Doctor. What a pleasure to see you. You are the reason for Garrett's last-minute trip to London, I presume?"

"Yes, he came to extend an invitation to the wedding. I do apologize for this very late arrival, but something urgent came up. I hope you will allow Garrett a chance to explain."

"Of course we will," Devon replied. "Please, everyone, come inside."

As they made their way to the door, Charlotte turned to Dr. Thomas and held out her hand. "I am so happy to see you, sir."

He cupped her hand inside both of his, and his eyes glimmered with warmth. "I am happy to see you, too, my dear. Merry Christmas."

"I have a present for you," Charlotte said with a grin.

"And I have something for you as well."

Garrett realized he would have to catch up on the familiarity that existed between these two. He was not sorry, for it, however. It was something he would antici-pate with great joy.

Then he turned to Anne and hoped she would be willing to hear him out.

ღიღ

"You saved his life?" Anne said from clear across the drawing room.

Standing with his brothers around the Christmas tree, Garrett gestured toward Dr. Thomas, who stood in front of the mantel. "It was mostly the good doctor who did the saving."

"That is pure rubbish," Dr. Thomas replied. "I couldn't possibly have pulled that boy out of the water and carried him all the way back to the coach through the deep snow as you did. You were the hero of the day long before I withdrew my stethoscope."

"Sounds like it was a shared effort," Devon said, raising his cup of hot cider for an informal toast. Blake raised his cup as well.

Anne smiled at Garrett, for she, more than anyone else in the room, understood what it must have meant for him to save that boy's life. He had come home to Pembroke seeking to atone for quite another tragedy, and perhaps this unexpected Christmas Eve ordeal had provided him some relief and validation for what he had not been able to accomplish in the past.

Everyone gathered around the tree, except for Anne, who remained at the sofa. They all raised their cups and toasted the boy's recovery, as well as Garrett's safe return.

But there was another glaring issue to which no one had yet alluded. The will ... The family fortune ...

Garrett finished his cider and set down his cup. "What happened with Father last night? Was he very distraught when the wedding did not take place?"

"We were all distraught," Adelaide replied, "but mostly because we were worried about you. But your father ..." She paused. "He didn't seem to realize that it was Christmas Eve, or that your wedding was scheduled to take place. Of course none of us said anything. He fell asleep early and slept through most of the storm. I checked on him this morning and he ate a small breakfast, then ordered a hot bath."

Garrett regarded his mother with relief. "Thank heavens for that. I was very concerned last night. I know how anxious he can be."

"Some days are worse than others," his mother replied. "Yesterday was a good day."

Everyone stood quietly for a moment until Garrett finally broached the subject of the will, and the wedding that did not take place. "Will you fight the terms?" he asked Devon. "Try to keep our family fortune intact?"

"I've had lawyers working on it for months," Devon replied, "and I will continue to do what I can. Now that the deadline has passed, however, I am not sure what hope there will be. We must all prepare ourselves for reduced circumstances."

Charlotte sighed heavily. "Then I suppose it will be up to me to refill the family coffers. Perhaps I will run off to America and marry a rich railroad tycoon who wants to purchase our family name for his business interests."

The duchess slid an arm around her waist. "Only if he's handsome, dear."

Everyone chuckled, except for Anne, who was not sure what role she would play in this family's new future. She had not been able to fulfill her contract with Garrett and secure the Pembroke fortune. She would therefore not receive the compensation that had been promised to her—the compensation that would have ensured her independence.

But what would Garrett *want*? she wondered as she listened to him describe how grateful Marcus and Joshua's parents had been when they arrived to collect the boys that morning. They had wept tears of joy as they thanked Garrett and Dr. Thomas.

Anne was so happy for him, and so thankful that everything had worked out.

At last, Garrett told his family about his boating accident in the spring, and how he had not been able to save the passengers on board. "I came home seeking some form of atonement, but what I've learned is that nothing will ever erase what happened on the water that day. Nothing will take away the grief of those who were left behind. All I can do is try to remember that I did my best to save them, and that in the future, I will find ways to be useful and helpful in this life. Yesterday, it took all of us to bring that boy back from disaster. Not one of us could have done it alone. It was a shared effort." He paused. "I do not believe I am meant to be alone."

"No, you are not." The duchess took hold of his hand and kissed it with all the love and compassion Anne knew she would provide, if only Garrett would open up to her and the rest of his family.

Garrett met Anne's eyes just then and gazed at her for a tortuous moment while she tried to read his thoughts about their future together, but it was no use. She was lost in a haze of longing and desire.

"Anne." he said in front of everyone. "You, more than anyone, deserve my most heartfelt apologies for keeping you waiting last night. How can I ever make it up to you?"

She looked down at the floor. "That is not necessary, Garrett. You and Dr. Thomas have explained why you could not be here. It could not be helped and I am so happy you were able to help those boys. I certainly bear no ill will."

Before she realized what was happening, Garrett had crossed the room and was down on one knee before her. She blinked down at him with surprise.

"This is something I must do in front of witnesses, Anne, and please listen carefully." He took hold of her hand. "I came home to Pembroke Palace a broken man, but in a very short time, you helped make me whole again—with your kindness, your understanding, and your beauty, inside and out. If I am not mistaken, my entire family has fallen in love with you, and I more than any of them cannot imagine a life without you here with all of us at Pembroke. I kneel down before you now, not to fulfill the terms of any contract or to act out a charade, but to satisfy my own heart, because I love you with every breath in my body."

She laid a hand over her own heart, fearing that it might stop beating.

But there was more. He still had more beautiful things to say.

"I want you for the rest of my life, Anne. I want you as my bride, and as the mother of my children. And there *will* be children, I guarantee it—a whole houseful of them—if you would but honor me with your hand."

Anne sucked in a breath and struggled to find her voice. Was this really happening?

Garrett smiled up at her with those dazzling blue eyes and said, "Will you marry me, Anne? For real? Never to be apart? Will you make me the happiest man alive?"

Overcome by a dizzying mixture of joy and disbelief, feeling as if she were caught in a glorious, heavenly dream, she reached out to run her hand over his thick, golden hair.

"You haven't answered me," he said with a confident, seductive smile.

She responded by tugging at the shoulders of his jacket to pull him to his feet. "You know I love you, Garrett, so how can there be any answer but *yes*?"

She was vaguely aware of the others cheering and applauding as he pulled her into his arms and pressed his mouth to hers for a passionate kiss that sent the whole world spinning.

His hands settled on the curve of her hips as he drew back and looked down at her dress. "You are already dressed for our wedding. Can we not do it now?"

Anne couldn't help herself. She laughed out loud and glanced at Charlotte, who was watching with wide, hopeful eyes.

"Say yes!" Charlotte shouted. "The vicar is still here. He couldn't leave in the storm last night. He is probably in the breakfast room by now. He already has all the papers prepared."

Anne's heart beat fast with excitement. "Am I dreaming?" she asked.

"No, by God, you are fully awake," Garrett replied, as he kissed her again with fierce, relentless passion. The touch of his lips seared her blood. Then he swept her into his arms like an eager groom about to cross the threshold on the wedding night.

It was the morning after, of course, but Anne was not about to split hairs. *Better late than never*, her mother always used to say.

She laughed out loud as her soon-to-be husband carried her out of the room to hunt down the vicar.

Chapter Eighteen

*L*ATER THAT AFTERNOON, Anne threw her head back in ecstasy as Garrett made love to her for the third time in the wedding chamber that had been prepared for them the day before.

Charlotte had placed rose petals between the sheets—clipped and stolen from the duke's prized conservatory. It was a briefly distracting but pleasant surprise when they slipped naked into bed.

Now they lay together in the fading light, talking about the private ceremony in the chapel.

"The duke seemed well," Anne said. "He was so happy for you, Garrett. How proud he looked when he shook your hand after the vicar pronounced us man and wife."

"That was all I ever wanted from him," Garrett replied. "Just a sign that he cared."

"I saw it very clearly today," she assured him, while she ran the tip of her finger across the smooth muscles of her husband's chest and reveled in the wonderful notion that she was no longer a social outcast. She had been accepted into this powerful aristocratic family, and had spoken vows before God in their beautiful chapel.

"And he didn't mention the curse," she added. "Not once. Do you think he has forgotten about it, or will he imagine it again the next time it rains or snows?"

"I'm not sure." Garrett gently stroked her shoulder and was quiet for a long time. "Do you ever wonder if he really is talking to ghosts?"

She sat up. "Why do you ask?"

He felt foolish bringing it up, but something his father said to him would not leave his mind. "After we found him in the catacombs last week, he told me that Brother Salvador said there was a reason I was not lost, and that it wasn't time for me to leave. I cannot help but wonder what Brother Salvador knows about my future."

Anne smiled tenderly at him. "I am sure time will tell all."

Garrett sighed and continued to stroke her shoulder. "Yes. We simply have to *live*. Seek out our destinies. In the meantime, I feel very blessed. And inspired."

She lifted her head and rested her chin on her hands. "About the future?"

"Yes. I know now that I want to enrol in Kings College to study medicine, if they will have me. I know it is not quite the proper thing for the son of a duke, but we must remember that I am actually the son of a doctor, and I feel compelled to follow in his footsteps. Perhaps that is my true destiny. I respect Dr. Thomas a great deal, Anne. He is a brilliant man."

"And your mother loved him once, didn't she."

"I suspect she loves him still," he replied, "but she will never again be unfaithful. I didn't tell you every detail of our conversation that day, but I wish to tell you now. She said that marriage is sacred, and she prayed that none of her children would ever feel a need to stray from their spouses—that we would marry the true mates of our souls and love each other until the end of time."

Anne thought about the duchess. "How sad that she did not marry the true mate of *her* soul."

Garrett pulled her closer into the warmth of his embrace. "I believe she has come to accept that sometimes, things happen for a reason—even difficult things. I also believe that despite everything, she loves her husband, and he loves her very much in return. Time has tempered the turmoil of their early years, and after almost losing her, he did become a better husband. But first and foremost, she is devoted to this family, each and every one of us."

"But poor Dr. Thomas," Anne said.

Garrett was quiet for a moment. "There is no doubt in my mind that he still loves my mother and always will. I believe he would walk through fire for her. He is a very honorable gentleman, selfless in every way."

Anne gazed lovingly into Garrett's eyes. "I would walk through fire for you as well. And I will have no problem living up to your mother's expectations of loving you selflessly, until the end of time. I will be very proud if you become a medical man. I cannot imagine a higher calling."

"Higher callings aside," he said with a flirtatious smile as he leaned up on an elbow, rolled her over onto her back, and kissed her collarbone. "We will no doubt need the money."

A knock sounded at the door. They both lifted their heads.

"Who in the world would be interrupting us *now*?" Garrett said.

"It must be important," Anne suggested.

Garrett laid a quick kiss on her breast. "Don't move. Do not leave this bed. I will be back in an instant."

"I assure you," she replied as she watched him shrug into his robe, "I have no desire to go anywhere."

He crossed the room, opened the door a crack, and peered out. Anne heard him say, "This better be important. We're rather busy at the moment."

There was some whispering, and Garrett glanced over his shoulder at her.

Anne sat up in the bed.

Garrett slipped out into the corridor.

Hastily, she reached for her dressing gown and padded to the open door.

Garrett was standing in the hall with Devon and Blake. They appeared to be looking over a document.

"What's going on?" she asked.

They all turned to look at her. No one moved. Garrett looked stricken with shock.

"This is quite unbelievable," he said. "I am not sure what to make of it."

Anne strode a little closer to look at the document. He held it up to the light from the window at the end of the corridor.

"Is this our wedding certificate?" she asked.

"Yes. It's dated yesterday."

Startled by the implications that flashed through her mind, she squinted to look at it more closely.

Devon inclined his head at her. "To be clear, we do not believe the vicar was trying to commit fraud. He must have prepared all the papers yesterday and forgot to change the dates."

Anne laid her hand on Garrett's shoulder. "What does this mean? Will you submit these papers to the solicitors?"

The brothers regarded each other warily.

"That would be dishonest," Blake said.

"It would be pure madness," Garrett added. "But no more mad than the curse that will somehow, ridiculously, hold up in court if we scratch out those dates and tell the truth."

Anne frowned with concern. "What about the duke? He watched us get married today. What if he tells someone?"

"I don't think he even knows what day it is," Devon replied. "Today he was happier than I've ever seen him. The curse was the last thing on his mind. I'm not sure if he even remembers that he bequeathed his fortune to the Horticultural Society."

Anne and Garrett locked gazes. "It is not my decision," she said to him. "This is *your* fortune, you and your brothers."

His shoulders rose and fell with a deep breath. "God knows, if I had it, I would put it to good use."

He was referring to the fund he wished to bestow upon Georgina's parents. And his mother's charities. And Kings College.

"I wish Vincent were here," Devon said.

Blake looked over the marriage certificate very carefully. "He doesn't need to be here. We all know what he would say." He tapped a finger on the seal. "No one can deny this is a legal document. So is the license."

"So we should simply submit it to the solicitors, say nothing, and let them deal with it?" Garrett surmised.

They all looked to one another for clarification.

"That seems the proper thing," Devon said.

Another moment of silence ensued.

Blake patted Garrett on the back. "Good heavens. We have disturbed your wedding celebrations. Incidentally it's almost time to dress for dinner. Devon and I must go."

Anne watched her brothers-in-law make haste toward the east wing. She then discreetly tiptoed back into the cozy bedchamber where the fire was blazing, and waited for Garrett to close the door behind him.

With his eyes closed, he leaned against it and tipped his head back. "Another Christmas miracle." He lifted his head and regarded her with an intense look of lust in his eye. "This is because of you, isn't it? You truly are an angel sent from heaven."

Anne's eyebrows lifted, then she burst out laughing. Garrett ripped off his robe, ran naked toward her and scooped her into his arms. She screeched with a boisterous trill as he carried her back to the bed for a few more enjoyable miracles before the sun went down and it was time for Christmas dinner—which promised to be a most delectable meal.

"I can't believe how much I love you," he said, as he smiled down at her and showered her with hot, deliciously wicked kisses.

She held him tight in her arms, thanked God for the incredible gift of this man in her life, and wondered recklessly how long they could go without eating.

Dear Reader,

Thank you so much for reading MARRIED BY MIDNIGHT, the fourth instalment in my Pembroke Palace series—which was a long time coming. It is now 2012, and book number three (WHEN A STRANGER LOVES ME) was published in 2009. I apologize for the wait, but I hope it was worth it! I certainly enjoyed writing Garrett's story ... finally.

If you are interested in reading the other books in the series (all full length novels), here they are in chronological order:

IN MY WILDEST FANTASIES (Devon and Rebecca)
THE MISTRESS DIARIES (Vincent and Cassandra)
WHEN A STRANGER LOVES ME (Blake and Chelsea)

Charlotte's story is in the works and I am aiming for a release in 2013. I don't have a title yet, but if you would like to stay informed about the exact release date and be the first to see the cover art, please visit my website at www.juliannemaclean.com and sign up for my mailing list. I would love to send news to you.

Best wishes and happy reading!

Julianne MacLean

Books by Julianne MacLean

Harlequin Historical Romances:
Prairie Bride
The Marshal and Mrs. O'Malley
Adam's Promise

The American Heiress Series:
To Marry the Duke
An Affair Most Wicked
My Own Private Hero
Love According to Lily
Portrait of a Lover
Surrender to a Scoundrel

The Pembroke Palace Series:
In My Wildest Fantasies
The Mistress Diaries
When a Stranger Loves Me
Married By Midnight

The Highlander Trilogy:
Captured by the Highlander
Claimed by the Highlander
Seduced by the Highlander
The Rebel (A Highlander Short Story)

The Royal Trilogy:
Be My Prince
Princess in Love
The Prince's Bride

Contemporary Fiction
Writing as E.V.Mitchell:
The Color of Heaven

About the Author

Julianne MacLean is a USA Today bestselling author of 15 historical romances, including The Highlander Trilogy with St. Martin's Press and her popular American Heiress series with Avon/Harper Collins. She also writes contemporary mainstream fiction under the pseudonym E.V. Mitchell, and her most recent release THE COLOR OF HEAVEN was an Amazon bestseller. She is a three-time RITA finalist, and has won numerous awards, including the Booksellers' Best Award, the Book Buyers Best Award, and a Reviewers' Choice Award from Romantic Times for Best Regency Historical of 2005. She lives in Nova Scotia with her husband and daughter, and is a dedicated member of Romance Writers of Atlantic Canada. Please visit the author's website for more information.

Praise for Julianne MacLean...

"You can always count on Julianne MacLean to deliver ravishing romance that will keep you turning pages until the wee hours of the morning."   —Teresa Medeiros

"Julianne MacLean's writing is smart, thrilling, and sizzles with sensuality."   —Elizabeth Hoyt

"Scottish romance at its finest, with characters to cheer for, a lush love story, and rousing adventure. I was captivated from the very first page. When it comes to exciting Highland romance, Julianne MacLean delivers."
     —Laura Lee Guhrke

"She is just an all-around, wonderful writer and I look forward to reading everything she writes."
     —Romance Junkies

The Highlander Trilogy

Bestselling author Julianne MacLean unleashes
the epic passions of three Highland warriors
who won't go down without a fight—and will
take no prisoners in the name of love . . .

Captured by the Highlander

Lady Amelia Sutherland would rather die than surrender to a man like Duncan MacLean. He is the fiercest warrior of his clan—her people's sworn enemy—and tonight he is standing over her bed. Eyes blazing, muscles taut, and battle axe gleaming, MacLean has come to kill Amelia's fiancé. But once he sees the lovely, innocent Amelia, he decides to take her instead ...

Stealing the young bride-to-be is the perfect revenge against the man who murdered Duncan's one true love. But Lady Amelia turns out to be more than a pawn of vengeance and war. This brave, beautiful woman touches something deep in Duncan's soul that is even more powerful than a warrior's fury. But when Amelia begins to fall in love with her captor—and surrenders in his arms—the real battle begins ...

Claimed by the Highlander

With his tawny mane, battle-hewn brawn, and ferocious roar, Angus "The Lion" MacDonald is the most fearsome warrior Lady Gwendolen has ever seen—and she is his most glorious conquest. Captured in a surprise attack on her father's castle, Gwendolen is now forced to share her bed with the man who defeated her clan. But, in spite of Angus's overpowering charms, she refuses to surrender her innocence without a fight . . .

With her stunning beauty, bold defiance, and brazen smile , Gwendolen is the most infuriating woman Angus has ever known—and the most intoxicating. Forcing her to become his bride will unite their two clans. But conquering Gwendolen's heart will take all his skills as a lover. Night after night, his touch sets her on fire. Kiss after kiss, his hunger fuels her passion. But, as Gwendolen's body betrays her growing love for Angus, a secret enemy plots to betray them both . . .

Seduced by the Highlander

War, Lachlan MacDonald has conquered so many men on the battlefield—and so many women in the bed-room—that he is virtually undefeated. But one unlucky tryst with a seductive witch has cursed him forever. Now, any women he makes love to will be doomed for eternity ...

Lady Catherine is a beautiful lass of elite origin—or so she is told. Suffering from amnesia, she is desperate to find the truth about who she really is ... or, at the very least, meet someone who inspires an intense memory or emotion. When she first lays eyes on Lachlan MacDonald, Catherine has a sixth sense that he holds the key that will unlock her past—and maybe even her heart. But how could she know that the passion she ignites in this lusty warrior's heart could consume—and destroy—them both?

CPSIA information can be obtained at www.ICGtesting.com
Printed in the USA
LVOW050035180912

299171LV00001B/325/P